The Spreewald Collection

Also by Donald MacKenzie

Occupation: Thief
Manhunt
The Juryman
Scent of Danger
Dangerous Silence
Knife Edge
The Genial Stranger
Double Exposure
Cool Sleeps Balaban
The Lonely Side of the River
Salute from a Dead Man
Death Is a Friend
The Quiet Killer
Dead Straight
Night Boat from Puerto Vedra
The Kyle Contract
Sleep Is for the Rich
Postscript to a Dead Letter
Zaleski's Percentage

Donald MacKenzie

The Spreewald Collection

Houghton Mifflin Company Boston

c 10 9 8 7 6 5 4 3 2

Library of Congress Cataloging in Publication Data

MacKenzie, Donald, 1908-
The spreewald collection.

(Midnight novel of suspense) I. Title.
PZ4.M1562Sp [PR9199.3.M325] 813'.5'4 74-20706
ISBN 0-395-20286-8

Printed in the United States of America

For Jonathan and Sue Guinness
in appreciation of their friendship

Author's Note

This story was finished in Portugal a few days before the events of April 25, 1974. I have tried to portray a way of life and a system of government that lasted for forty-eight years, unique in the history of Portugal and unlikely to be re-created. My wish is that those who now determine the fate of this kindly and often misunderstood people will be equal to their task.

D.M

Albufeira, Portugal
July 23, 1974

The Spreewald Collection

I

IT WAS EVENING and a dense fog had descended on the jail buildings, obscuring the boundary walls and making watery balloons of the lamps in the exercise yards. The prison grounds were deserted, the dog-handlers still sheltering in the warders' mess. Inside the cellblocks it was bedlam. The glass-roofed halls echoed with shouted instructions and the ringing of bells as men were unlocked for classes or association.

Hamilton lay on his back on the coconut-fiber mattress, his feet up against the wall. Washed-blue eyes, a humorous mouth and a nose broken by a flying hockey puck gave him a look of cheerful belligerence. His toffee-colored hair was streaked with gray and worn longer than it had been for the past three years. He reached for the makings and rolled himself a loose cigarette, indifferent to the noise outside his cell. He'd heard it all before, one thousand and ninety-four times. He hardened his stomach muscles and felt them confidently. For a man who had done his time the hard way he was in good shape. The press-ups and knee-bends had paid off. The habit was twenty-five years old. There had been little opportunity for sloth or sex at St. Columba's, though the Christian Brothers had searched hard for both.

The cellblocks were quiet again now. The chapel clock struck half-past six. His practiced ear detected the slither of felt-soled slippers outside his door. The hack on patrol lifted the cover of the spyhole, producing a disembodied eye that stared into the cell. Hamilton stuck two fingers in the air. The spyhole cover dropped. Four cellblocks formed a cross with a glass-enclosed booth at the point of intersection. This was the nerve center of the jail. Alarm calls registered on a panel there sending the strong-arm squads on standby duty rushing out to the yards or workshops. The cells nearest the center were occupied by men on A Escape List, high security risks. Below them were the Punishment Cells, an off-limit area reached by a flight of notorious stairs. It was a place of permanent twilight where prisoners purged their offenses against discipline in solitary confinement. Hamilton had spent most of his first year down there among the bedbugs and cracked water pipes, achieving a local record of eighteen appearances in front of the Governor, always on the same charge. Colonel Bullen ran a lockstep jail on the premise that the way to deal with first offenders was to hit them hard and often. There was no room for noncomformists in the Colonel's scheme of things and Hamilton's stubborn defiance offended him deeply. Refusal to obey an order amounted to mutiny in the Colonel's eyes. The punishment was standard, loss of remission of sentence, loss of privileges and dietary punishment. Number One Diet consisted of a pound of bread a day and as much water as the jug held. The only reading matter allowed was denominational prayer books. Atheists and agnostics had to make out with the *Statutory Rules for Convicted Prisoners.*

When Hamilton made his eighteenth appearance, Colonel Bullen made some inquiries about his recalcitrant charge. He learned that other than this dogged refusal to share a cell Hamilton's behavior was exemplary. He made no complaints, accepting castigation with a levity that nonplused the hard-nosed heavies in charge of the punishment cells. Colonel took time out to explain. British prisons were overcrowded. With certain exceptions it was necessary to house three men in a cell. Hamilton was neither a homosexual nor an escape risk, and the Medical Officer said that his lungs were sound. There was no valid reason why the rules should not apply to him as well as to others. The Canadian's answer had been brief and courteous. The last time he had slept in a room with members of his own sex had been in reform school. He had no intention of repeating the experience. It was a contest in which both men thought they had won. Hamilton certainly finished in a single cell but he served every day of his time.

He shifted his feet on the wall, looking around at the room's meager contents. Someone else would be laying out this crap tomorrow, the bedboard against the wall, the blankets and sheets neatly folded. There was not one thing of his own to take to Reception in the morning. No letters, no photographs. Except for Kohn's weekly visits it was three years to the day since he'd had contact with the outside world.

A key fumbled in the lock and a massive head peered around the door. "May I come in?"

It was Trueblue Kohn and the opening dialogue never varied.

"Be my guest," said Hamilton.

Kohn eased his big body into the cell, clutching his homburg to his chest. He never failed to observe the courtesies, asking permission to sit before spreading his fat buttocks on the stool. His silver hair was cunningly arranged to conceal a bald patch. A fleshy nose drooped between mournful Labrador eyes. He was expensively dressed with neat small feet stuffed into handmade shoes. After thirty-three years in the country his accent still betrayed his German origin.

"So here it is finally! Our last visit together."

Hamilton rolled himself another butt. The way he was going, the half-ounce of tobacco he had hoarded wouldn't be enough for the night.

"I didn't know if you'd be able to make it with this fog and all. But then, you never let me down."

Kohn's fingers made a fluttering movement of deprecation. "It would take more than fog. You have no idea how much I have profited from these visits."

The coarse-cut tobacco was burning unevenly. Hamilton licked the paper.

"You've got to be kidding!"

"No," said Kohn. "You have reassured me about many things. The power of an obstinate mind for one."

Hamilton's shoulders sagged a couple of inches on the whitewash. "You know what the Governor calls it? Excessive self-esteem! He gave me some farewell advice this morning. He warned me against the sin of pride."

Kohn picked at his ear delicately. "And what about the summons to Canada House?"

Hamilton made a face. "Nothing more. I don't think he *knows* any more. Just that I'm supposed to go to the High Commissioner's office first thing in the morning."

Kohn inspected the fluff on his fingernail. "Shall you go?"

"I guess so," said Hamilton. "It's probably something to do with my passport. These jokers have been trying to take it away from me for years."

Kohn's face was concerned. "Can they do that?"

"No way," shrugged Hamilton. "It still has three years to run."

Kohn digested the news thoughtfully. "How much do you know about the Prison Visitors scheme, Scott?"

Hamilton leaked smoke from the side of his mouth. "Not much. I asked around when you wanted me put on your list. Some of the guys here have you people figured for cranks. Me, I've been grateful for what you've offered."

The shadow lengthened on the wall as Kohn's head lifted. "They gave me six records to read when I first came here. I felt ashamed, a peeping Tom. Yours was one of them."

"Don't worry about it," grinned Hamilton. "Mine must have been a mind-bender. Altar boy to burglar in twenty-four easy lessons."

A certain stiltedness came into the older man's manner. "There was something about it that set it apart from the others. It seemed to me that if anyone could help me understand, it would be you."

"Understand *what?*" asked Hamilton. He filled another paper with tobacco. "Me, I hadn't seen a face I wanted to remember in two years. When you're that far down you'll grab at anything. The guys rapped on about how you people sneaked in the odd piece of contraband. You were a disappointment to me there, Philip. Not even a salt-beef sandwich!" He smiled to take the sting out of the words. In fact, what Kohn had provided was far more important than a couple of joints or a slug of Scotch. He'd been a link with a world removed from the sour stench of prison, a token of freedom.

Kohn placed his hands on his knees, his voice low and urgent. "I need you, Scott. I need you to burgle a house for me. I'll give you three thousand pounds."

Hamilton sat up straight as someone dragged a bed-board overhead. He felt like a man who has just been propositioned at a PTA meeting.

"I think I'll make out I never heard that," he said softly.

Kohn leaned forward. "I'm serious, Scott. I'm not asking you to do something dishonest. The property I want you to retrieve is mine."

"Why me?" demanded Hamilton.

"I need an expert. The house is well protected. And it has to be someone I can trust."

Hamilton used another match to relight the moist tobacco. "You mean to tell me that you've been coming in here for over a year, setting me up for this?"

Kohn's fingers gripped Hamilton's knee with surprising force. "No! Something happened a couple of months ago, something that has affected my whole life. I know you don't believe in justice, Scott, but how about retribution?"

"I'm not bigoted," Hamilton said staring at his visitor. "OK, I'll buy it. You're not drunk. You're just a respectable citizen putting a dishonest suggestion to a man who's seen the light. Doesn't it occur to you that you're taking a bit of a chance?"

Kohn's brown eyes filled with certainty. "No. You are neither an informer nor a blackmailer. Will you help me, Scott?"

Hamilton's shoulders resumed their original position against the wall.

"The man asks if I'll help him! Look, Philip, I'm broke and three thousand pounds is a lot of bread. It's the thought of going to jail again that scares the hell out of me."

Kohn was his urbane self again. "There will be help and the risks will be minimized."

Hamilton laughed out loud. "You're incredible, you really are! You've been doing this cool number with me, the refugee boy who made good, and now this! You know, it's kind of confusing."

"You don't trust me?"

"I'm baffled," said Hamilton. "No moral objections, just plain baffled."

A bell rang in the distance. Kohn turned his wrist, consulting a coin-thin watch on a platinum strap.

"Time's up. I have to go. At least think about what I have said and telephone me in the morning. Will you do that?" He rose, his bulk making the cell seem even smaller.

Hamilton pushed up off the wall. "Sure. I'll call you, Philip."

Kohn struck his hand out. "I hope you will. I'm counting on you." The door closed behind him.

Hamilton slipped off his shoes, rolled yet another cigarette and started padding from the door to the window and back. Jail was a great place for propositions. Nearly everyone had a tale of a safe left unattended, of loot buried in some lonely place, the rich businessman ready and ripe for a con. The tales were ninety-nine percent fiction, concocted from rumor and wishful thinking. But Kohn was a dealer in jade, a philanthropist, a solid citizen. Hamilton switched his thoughts. For three years he'd been no more than a cipher to be included in the daily lockup total. Suddenly his future was a matter of concern to the authorities. Governor, Chaplain, the guy from the After-Care Association, they'd all come on with the same stereotyped homilies. The courtroom flicked into perspective, the trial judge's face yellow in the globed lamps, a horsehair wig clamped low on his outthrust head. There'd been no bullshit in that preamble.

You'll go to prison, of course, Hamilton. I don't think

that anyone who has listened to the evidence would expect otherwise. Counsel has made the point that you used no violence. That may well be true. You are, nevertheless, a skilled and determined criminal, a first offender in name only. I'm fairly certain in my mind that this means no more than that it happens to be the first occasion on which you were caught. I'm going to give you the opportunity for self-appraisal though I am doubtful you will avail yourself of it. One can only hope. Three years' imprisonment!

Hamilton was still walking long after the lights went out. When the chapel clock struck eleven, he carried his chair to the window and stood on it, looking out through the bars. The fog was lifting on a strong wind. He could see the boundary walls glistening in the light of the arc lamps. A guard dog barked somewhere once, then the yards were silent. He undressed and made his bed for the last time. *The last time!* The words had a magic all their own.

Morning came surprisingly soon. He washed, shaved and was sitting ready by the time the day shift came on duty. Bedboards thudded up against the walls, porridge and tea cans clanged on the iron staircase. The jail was preparing for another day but this time without him. The door opened. He picked up his pillowcase. Inside were his library books and sheets. His escort was a youngster fresh from the army, wearing his cap at a rakish angle and smelling strongly of aftershave. He plucked Hamilton's card from the board outside the cell door and checked the details.

"Scott Hamilton? You due for discharge today?"

"Overdue," said Hamilton. "Let's get the hell out of here."

He followed the man along the gallery, deaf to the mock cheers and catcalls. There wasn't a face in a cell he wanted to see again. The deserted exercise yards were damp under a wan February sun. The fog had cleared completely. They walked past cabbages growing between concentric circles of concrete. The escort unlocked the gate leading to the Reception Block. His voice belonged to the parade ground.

"One prisoner for discharge, sir!"

A lifetime seemed to have gone by since Hamilton had stepped into the same long bare room. The Central Criminal Courts had sat late and it had been dark by the time the Black Maria reached the prison. Rain was lashing the desolate yards and cellblocks. They'd filed in, handcuffed, and sat on the wooden benches, each man standing as his name and sentence was read from the sheaf of committal orders.

"Scott Hamilton, three years' imprisonment!"

He remembered the sound of the rain outside, the smell of disinfectant, the emptiness in his mind as time-without-end stretched out in front of him.

He dropped his pillowcase in front of the desk. The hack in charge of Reception was a dyspeptic ex-sailor who occasionally did duty in the punishment cells. He leaned hard on his elbows, shaking his head with mock surprise.

"Stone the crows, it's Cheerful Charlie! I never thought I'd live to see the day. *Redband!*"

A rat-faced trusty wearing a red band on his sleeve scuttled in and removed the pillowcase. The hack licked a film of bicarbonate from the edges of his mouth. He emptied a small canvas bag onto the desk and checked its contents against the entries in the property book.

"One yeller metal watch! One wallet containing various papers! One Canadian passport and that's your lot! How much cash you got?"

Hamilton knew the amount by heart. "Eighty-seven pounds and fourteen shillings."

The warder rapped himself on the breastbone. "There you go, dropping yourself in it right away. All them birds'll know you've just left the nick. It's pence now, mate, not shillings. Eighty-seven quid and seventy pence. Sign here and get your clothes off."

Hamilton stood naked with his arms and legs outstretched. The hack pushed his fingers through the Canadian's hair.

"Open your mouth!"

Hamilton yawned and the hack peered inside. "Now bend over and keep 'em spread. No messages or prison property stuffed up there, is there?"

Hamilton straightened his back. The British had a talent for imposing the ultimate indignities. He moved toward the row of open cubicles. His civilian clothes were in the end one. The blue flannel suit and silk shirt had been pressed, his leather overcoat was neatly folded on the bench. The canvas bag on the floor held the remnants of his wardrobe. One pair of pajamas, a couple of shirts and some socks, the things he had taken to jail with him. He'd never known what had happened to the rest of his belongings. The vultures had swooped the moment he had been arrested, emptying the rented apartment. An occupational hazard, as Superintendent Cain had put it. His clothes smelled of camphor. He used the small square of mirror to knot the wide Cerruti tie. The hack leaned on his desk, watching the performance sardonically.

"Count it," he said, pushing the money across the desk when Hamilton came from the cubicle.

"I trust you," said Hamilton. "It's the expression in your eyes." He put the bills in his wallet, the change in his leather coat. He was the only prisoner to be released that day and the rat-faced trusty was out of sight. Hamilton beamed. "I'm glad it was you to see me off, Willy. Your delicacy has made all the difference."

"Up yours," grunted the jailer. "I know your kind. You'll be back for a certainty!"

Hamilton closed his right eye. "Don't hold your breath. And take good care of those ulcers!"

The hack half-grinned and bawled for the trusty. The man slid in, jockeying a polishing mop.

"Keep your thieving hands out of my pockets!" warned the jailer. He locked the top of his desk and waddled in front of Hamilton as far as the main gate. He rattled his key along the bars and shouted.

"One for the fleshpots!"

The massive front gates were opened only to wheeled traffic. A coal fire was burning in an office on the left. Hamilton could see the rows of keys waiting to be collected by the men returning on the breakfast shift.

The gate hack looked at Hamilton with frank curiosity. "There's someone waiting for you outside."

Hamilton's blood pressure jumped. He had grown to learn how fantasy permeates a prison, coloring the drab lives of the men who live there. The past and the present become unreal, only the future holds validity. Cons dream on, scrubbing floors, digging, stitching away at burlap bags, projecting their minds beyond the barrier of bitter reality. His own fantasy had always been that he'd walk out through these gates and there sitting behind the wheel of a car would be Mariga. She'd have a velvet beret pulled down low over her sleek black head and her violet eyes would be soft. The fashion photographers she modeled for had a name for her, Mariga the Resplendent. He'd look at her for one long last moment before lowering the boom and emptying his mind of her forever. Only then would the ghost be really laid.

He took a fresh hold on the canvas bag and stepped through the wicket gate to freedom. The asphalt concourse in front of the jail glistened in the pale sun. The entrance to the Governor's gloomy Gothic mansion was dwarfed by overgrown laurel bushes. Some children were waiting at the bus stop a hundred yards away. A car was parked under the elms between the front gates and the bus stop. Someone sounded the horn softly. It was too far to see the face behind the windshield but he hurried forward, adrenalin pumping into his veins. He recognized the bloomed windows at the back too late, the pipe in the mouth of the driver. The nearside rear door opened and he heard a familiar voice.

"Superintendent Cain. Remember me?"

Hamilton leaned into the car. "Why wouldn't I remember you?"

The flat planes of Cain's face appeared to be carved from a block of well-seasoned walnut. He wore no hat.

Thin sandy hair, bold brogues and a thick tweed suit gave an impression of a farmer on vacation. His eyes were the color of a beer bottle. He patted the seat beside him invitingly.

Hamilton looked away to the driver. The man winked up into the mirror. Hamilton shook his head in disbelief.

"I just can't believe what I'm seeing."

Cain had a way of snapping his teeth before he spoke, like a terrier taking a tentative bite.

"Jump in," he said. "And shut the door."

"What for?" asked Hamilton. "What's on your mind? I have things to do."

The lower half of Cain's face creaked into a grin. "Come on now, you know the drill. Get in. It won't take long."

Their stares locked for a second. Hamilton was the first to break. He threw his bag on the back seat. The door slammed shut and the car moved forward, turning left into the eastbound traffic. Cain plucked at a ginger hair in his left nostril, his tone chatty.

"What's the matter with you, for crissakes? What are you so nervous about?"

They were traveling fast as if the driver knew exactly where he was going. Hamilton cleared his throat and answered with feeling.

"I'll tell you what's the matter with me. I'm sitting in a goddamn police car, that's what's the matter with me!"

Cain aimed his voice at the back of the driver's head. "There's gratitude for you, Bill."

The pipe-smoker grunted noncommittally.

"I didn't want to put you on show," Cain explained. "That's why I did it this way."

"Did *what* this way?" requested Hamilton. The police car overtook a bus. Blank faces stared out through the steamed windows. He could see children milling around in a wired-off playground, a man taking down the shutters in front of a pawnshop. He had an odd feeling of unreality as if all this were happening to somebody else.

Cain nodded cheerfully. "We're going to the Chelsea nick."

"I'm going nowhere," Hamilton burst out. His fingers found the door catch. "You can let me out right here!"

Cain reached across and knocked up Hamilton's arm. "Don't make a bleeding fool of yourself. Half an hour and you'll be on your way. There's something I want to show you."

Hamilton sagged back on his seat. It was the nightmare of every con! They busted you as you hit the street and charged you with some old offense. But they weren't supposed to do that in England. Short of a crime like murder, a trial and sentence was meant to wipe the slate clean. So what in hell was Cain playing at?

"I'm due at Canada House about now," Hamilton said in a level voice. "And if I don't show, people are going to be asking questions."

"You'll be there," Cain said easily. "This is only a friendly talk."

"I've had enough friendly talks to last me a lifetime," Hamilton answered. He stared suspiciously, getting up tighter by the minute. The driver took his hand from the wheel and rapped his pipe into the ashtray. The traffic was dense as they neared Hammersmith Broadway. They stopped at the signals. Cain leaned forward.

"I'd take Fulham, Bill."

The driver nodded. A woman in a sports model alongside turned her head, looking absently at the bloomed windows of the police car.

"I don't think you like me," Cain remarked suddenly.

"Shit," said Hamilton. "What the hell *is* all this anyway?"

Cain consulted a round nickel watch. "Old Brompton Road, Bill. The back doubles should be clear by now." He picked at his nose again, his bottle-brown eyes quizzical. "They tell me you did your time the hard way."

"That's a matter of opinion," answered Hamilton. "Look, if this is a pinch you're supposed to tell me."

Cain wagged his rusty head. "We don't do that sort of thing in England. You know that, Scott. I've already told you, this is just a friendly chat."

The car accelerated, turned south and sped east again. It slowed, filtering through the one-way streets behind the hospitals on Fulham Road. It was barely half-after-nine and most of the stores on Chelsea Green were still closed. The red-brick apartment building where Hamilton had once lived towered over the modern police station that angled the junction of two streets. The driver braked in front of the station-house steps.

"Thanks, Bill."

Cain signaled Hamilton to get out. It was thirty-eight months since he'd walked up these steps and he remembered the occasion clearly. The fat desk sergeant who had booked him, the drunk yelling in the cell next door, the hollow sound of feet on the staircase. They climbed the dusty stairs and Cain opened the door of the C.I.D. room. A plainclothesman sitting at a desk held up his thumb.

"Battersea just called about the Chelsea Square job. They fished the safe out of the drink an hour ago. Empty, no dabs."

"What did they expect?" Cain asked bleakly. "A signed confession? How about taking a walk?"

The plainclothesman looked up at Hamilton. His eyes were thoughtful.

"A long walk or a short walk?"

"Twenty minutes," said Cain. He waited till the door had shut and shoved a chair in Hamilton's direction.

The room was shabby in the winter sunshine. The plain deal desks were littered with papers, the pattern had been worn off the linoleum on the floor, lists of WANTED notices and stolen property hung on the wall beneath an institutional clock. A two-bar heater burned in front of the empty fire grate. Cain opened a drawer in a desk.

"How about a cup of tea?"

Hamilton shook his head and sat down. A Black Maria had drawn up in the yard beneath the windows.

"Take a look at these," invited Cain. He lifted a bunch of skeleton keys on the end of a pencil. "Recognize them?"

A label was attached to the key ring. Hamilton swallowed hard, his mouth suddenly dry.

"So what?"

Cain read the inscription on the label. "Central Criminal Courts, Court Number Two, *Regina* v. *Hamilton*, Exhibit Number Seven. I've got you down on my list for twenty-nine jobs over a period of years, jobs you never admitted. I don't have to give you the names. You know them as well as I do. I only got you for one. You left all that other shit down to me."

Hamilton managed a careful smile. "Nobody wins them all."

"True," Cain said reflectively. His tone sharpened. "But I'm a bad loser. That's why I did my best to get you a seven. You were lucky. That judge must have fancied you."

Hamilton fished for a smoke and found none. The thought niggled at the back of his mind. Not even a chance to buy a pack of cigarettes.

"You didn't bring me here to tell me that," he observed.

Cain took a turn to the window. He stood for a while watching the night's haul of prisoners being loaded on their way to the courts. He swung around suddenly, arm outstretched and pointing at Hamilton.

"You're the kind of smart bastard I get a kick out of busting."

Hamilton blinked. "I got the message three years ago. If you're putting this on tape, watch your language."

Cain's wooden grin flapped open and shut. "Fuck you, Raffles! Did you ever work it out who shopped you?"

Hamilton shrugged. "You're the one who knows. You feed the pigeons."

Cain closed an eye, looking out along his nose. "One of your so-called friends. One of your jet-setting, check-bouncing friends."

Hamilton put a long-time hunch to the test. "Davey?"

"I'll let you sweat," said Cain. "The point is, what happens now, what are your plans?"

Hamilton laughed shortly. "Getting out of this goddamn country as fast as I can. Why?"

Cain's muddy eyes hooded briefly. He tore the exhibit label from the bunch of keys and threw it in the wastebasket.

"All gone! Exhibit Number Seven has been duly destroyed according to regulations. You want to know why I brought you here, Hamilton. I'll tell you. I brought you here to make you a promise." The keys swung from the pencil, clinking.

Hamilton licked his lips. "Are you sure you have to?"

Cain leaned forward and his face now was menacing. "The very first time I catch you on my manor I'm going to find these keys in your pocket. Then I'm going to put you away for ever and ever and ever. Is that quite clear to you?"

The taste in Hamilton's mouth was suddenly bitter. Cain's threat was easy enough to implement. Burglary tools used as exhibits were handed to the arresting officer for destruction but there was no check.

"Will that be all?" he asked.

Cain nodded expansively. "That'll be all. Like me to arrange a lift to Canada House? Think of it as a taxi ride."

"No, thanks. Someone might recognize me."

"Suit yourself," shrugged Cain. "By the way, I heard that your bird screwed you for your money. Ran away with some golf bum and went to Australia, is what I heard."

Hamilton hefted his overnight bag. "Sounds as though you have a great ear for hearing things. Don't waste your time looking for me. I won't be around."

Cain shook his sandy head. "You're a loser, Hamilton. A born loser."

"Crazy," said Hamilton as he looked back from the door. "Thanks for the friendly talk."

He hurried down the steps and out of the building before someone pulled him back and turned the key on him. Seconds later he was on a Number Eleven bus bound for Trafalgar Square. The girl in the window seat next to him had a pinched nose set in a dead-white face and green eyelids. Her appearance was made even more bizarre by a Moroccan wool cap, long cloak and platform shoes like orthopedic aids. Nevertheless she was young and he was a new man. He gave her a friendly wink.

"Get lost," she said in a tight clear voice and buried her nose in a shorthand primer. So much for freedom. Up to now he wasn't doing too well with it.

He dropped off the bus opposite Charing Cross Station, bought a newspaper and French cigarettes, tea and toast in a cafeteria. He hung time till it was ten o'clock, then walked back to Trafalgar Square. Some blacks in tribal costume were picketing South Africa House under the bored surveillance of a couple of young cops. Nothing much seemed to have changed. Tourists posed among the pigeons, the meth-drinkers were sleeping it off on the benches near the fountains, a Gay Lib apologist with a shaven head and monk's habit was handing out leaflets. Hamilton walked up the steps of the solid gray building on the southwest corner of the square. The girl at the reception desk was a freckle-faced redhead with a prairie accent. She scribbled his name on a piece of paper, flourishing the pen professionally.

"You don't happen to know who your appointment is with, Mr. Hamilton?"

He placed his overnight bag on top of the counter, shaking his head.

"It's probably some sort of lottery. The loser gets me."

"If you'd like to give me your address," she asked crisply.

He leaned across confidentially. "Her Majesty's Prison, Wormwood Scrubs."

Her crispness seemed to curl somewhat at the edges. "Look, I don't have time for games."

"No game," he assured her. "They'll tell you upstairs. Go ahead and try."

She spoke into the phone. Her face was thoughtful when she put the phone down.

"If you'd go on up, Mr. Hamilton. It's the third floor, second door on your left."

He put his hand on the blue canvas bag. She nodded and he lifted it over the counter. She was wearing a Black Watch tartan dress with a silver-buckled belt.

"You know my name," he said appreciatively. "How about telling me yours?"

It was a couple of seconds before she made up her mind how to answer.

"Alison Dundas."

"Alison Dundas," he repeated. "And what's a nice girl like you doing in a dump like this?"

Relaxed, she was ready to give as good as she got. "I just play the piano. I've no idea what goes on upstairs."

He leaned closer so that his face almost touched her hair. "Mmmm. The color of a maple leaf in September."

She touched the back of her head self-consciously. "Mr. Gautier's waiting for you."

"That's the story of my life," he grinned. "There's always a Mr. Gautier waiting. You're not mad at me, are you?"

Her face was cool but not unfriendly. "You'd know it if I was."

He looked back from the elevator but she was busy with her papers.

He thumbed the third-floor button, pleased with himself. Alison Dundas, the name had a romantic ring to it. He'd chat her up when he came down again, invite her out for a drink, somewhere quiet and elegant. If the spell held he'd buy her a candlelit dinner and walk her home to some shared apartment with sagging chairs and a hundred yards of faded chintz. If he kissed her hand at the end it would be all, a toned-down Lochinvar out of the west with only one thought in mind, to sit across the table from a woman and be kind to her.

The elevator stopped. He turned left and knocked on a door. The bright room was carpeted wall-to-wall in serviceable blue. A couple of easy chairs had been positioned in front of a window overlooking the fountains below. An orange tiffany-silk lampshade bloomed over a leather-topped desk. Hamilton closed the door quietly.

"Mr. Gautier?"

The lean balding man by the bookshelves was Hamilton's age, modishly dressed in a tailored pigskin jacket and tan velvet trousers. Over his head were portraits of the Queen and Trudeau. He managed to pick up a folder from the desk and wave Hamilton to a chair with the same motion.

"How about a Canadian cigarette? I guess it's a long time since you tried one."

Hamilton dipped into the proffered box of British Consols. There was a framed snapshot of Gautier on the desk. It portrayed him sun-tanned, goggled and leaning on ski poles.

"It must have been rough in there?" Gautier asked pleasantly. Alpine sunshine had left his face burnished and brown. Hamilton blew out the match.

"Cigarettes, polite conversation. Things have been happening around here. Whatever happened to the Plague of the Prairies?"

Gautier smiled. "Jack Fogarty? He's in Washington. OK, you want to know why you're here, right?"

"Right," said Hamilton and leaned back.

Gautier opened his folder. "Does the name Ellis mean anything to you?"

Hamilton dribbled smoke from the corner of his mouth. "If it's Greg Ellis, yes. He's my mother's brother."

Gautier passed over a letter typed on business stationery.

ELLIS-JOHNSON SPECIALISTS IN OUTBOARD MOTORS
Light Craft Repairs Undertaken
Water Street
Kincardine Ontario

The High Commissioner for Canada
Canada House
Cockspur Street
London S.W.1.
England

Dear Sir,

I thank you for the information concerning my nephew Scott Hamilton. I understand from this that he will be released from prison on Feb. 11, 1974.

I want to point out that we live in a small community where the name of Scott's mother's family has always been respected. Because of this, his past behavior has caused all of us here considerable pain and embarrassment. With this in mind I am anxious to avoid the notoriety connected with Scott's deportation from England and hope that with your assistance it will be possible. I am enclosing my check for $500 (five hundred dollars) with the request that this money be used to pay Scott's passage back to Canada. Any excess could be applied to his expenses on the trip but on no account should my nephew be given this money for his own use.

Very truly yours,
Gregory Haig Ellis

Hamilton looked up. "The last time I heard of him was twenty years ago. It takes the threat of a headline in the Bruce County *Clarion* to bring Uncle Greg out of the woodwork."

Gautier pinned the check back on the letter. "It's a generous offer."

"Sure," said Hamilton. "Look, I lay in bed once with a compound fracture for nine weeks, marooned on the Gaspé Peninsula with a hard-nosed Highland hospital secretary clamoring for money every time the sheets were changed. Uncle Greg went stone-deaf. Lumberjacks earned good wages, he said. A young man with sense would have made provision against that kind of thing, he said, instead of blowing his paycheck with the riffraff of Montreal. The hospital threw me out. I still limp when it rains."

"It's a generous offer," Gautier repeated.

"With one basic flaw," pointed out Hamilton. "There's no deportation order out against me."

Gautier showed expensively capped teeth. "Come on, now. A technical oversight. You were lucky; you know it."

The suddenness of Hamilton's movement sent the pigeons fluttering from the windowsill.

"I'm beginning to detect a note of disapproval. What exactly is it that you people want of me?"

Gautier held up a hand in protest. "Hold it a minute! I'd never even heard of you till that file was dumped on my desk two weeks ago. But I know that you've hardly distinguished yourself over here."

"I know that too," answered Hamilton. "But I've no intention of going back to Canada, if that's what you mean. Not at the moment, anyhow."

Gautier tossed the folder back on the desk. "You could do a lot worse. Don't get me wrong. I don't give a personal damn what you do with your life. I'm simply passing on a comment from the Commissioner. He says, use your uncle's money and run for home."

Hamilton cocked his head. "Home?"

"You know what I mean," said Gautier.

Hamilton picked up his leather coat. "No way."

The official's lazy eyes narrowed. "I had a word with Scotland Yard yesterday. You're not winning any popularity contest there either. They'll cripple you next time."

"There isn't going to *be* a next time," said Hamilton.

Gautier spoke on the rise. "Well, it's your decision and I'll put it on record as such. There is one thing. You'll be dealing with me in the future and when the chips are down I'm a whole lot meaner than old Jack Fogarty. Don't come looking for favors."

"I won't," promised Hamilton. "It was good of you to give me your time." He left as quietly as he had entered. The girl downstairs had the blue canvas bag ready on the counter. She gave it to him, her eyes curious.

"Were you really in prison?" she asked softly.

He pulled his belt through the loops of his topcoat and buckled it. "You want to hear about it, have dinner with me tonight."

"A nice idea," she admitted. "But my husband wouldn't approve."

"I don't believe it," he challenged. "You're putting me on!"

She propped both elbows on the counter and smiled up at him. "It's true. He's there every night at five o'clock standing right where that Mountie is now. And I'm a very lucky girl."

He did his best to hide his disappointment. "There ought to be a law against it. Let me know if he doesn't treat you right."

"I'll do that," she said. "And take care!"

He held his smile for the RCMP trooper outside and made for the pay phones in the post office on the far side of the square. Kohn answered the call.

"You've got yourself a deal," Hamilton said tersely.

Kohn's tone brightened. "That's wonderful news. I'll admit I expected it but it's still good to hear." Hamilton caught the aside in German, then Kohn was back on the line. "There's someone I want you to meet. Can you come here now?"

"I'm on my way," said Hamilton. A taxi deposited him at the park end of Grosvenor Street.

He stood looking up at the red-brick façade of the Queen Anne house. The two windows on the first floor were shrouded in peach-colored silk. Brass fittings gleamed on the solid mahogany front door. Kohn's allusions to money had always been diffident and the air of opulent security came as a surprise to Hamilton. There were two bellpushes. He pressed the one marked PRIVATE. Kohn's voice issued from a bronze-framed speaker.

"Come on in, the door is open. The stairs are in front of you."

The room on the left of the paneled hallway was furnished in Regency style; a fire burned in an Adams grate. On the mantel above, an enormous jade horse reared back on its hindquarters, its polished blue-gray surface reflecting the flames. A woman was sitting in front of the fire with her back to Hamilton. Her dark hair was coiled on her neck and skewered with an ivory pin. She went on reading, not turning as he crossed to the white-painted staircase. The momentary collapse of the thick rug underfoot told him that he had trodden on a pressure pad. Kohn's face peered down from the head of the stairs. He was wearing a dark-gray suit with a rosebud in the lapel.

"So you noticed! I wondered if you would," he said. "The burglar-alarm system is wired directly to West London police station."

He reached to take Hamilton's bag and ushered him into a circular room at the head of the stairs. The walls were hung with bookshelves; more shelves were attached to the back of the door they had just come through. The effect was claustrophobic but it made for privacy. Kohn folded Hamilton's coat and draped it over a satinwood chest. He touched a button and a segment of the book-lined wall opened. The room they entered stretched from the front of the house to the back. Oriental rugs were strewn across a dull gold carpet, the velvet on the walls was a couple of shades brighter. The furniture was a mixture of periods and designs. Red-lacquered tables and chests, a Pleyel grand piano with a framed picture on top of the lid. Wedgwood vases, a Chinese scroll-table and a crimson leather couch with matching armchairs. The rear windows overlooked a patch of lawn. Three blue tits were swinging on a coconut suspended from an ornamental cherry tree. The room was like a set in some opulent stage production rather than a place where people lived.

A long-legged girl was sitting deep in one of the red chairs, staring at Hamilton with dark blue eyes tilted in a nervous sun-tanned face. Her sun-bleached hair was cropped short and she wore a checked gingham shirt under a yellow V-necked sweater. Her shoes were low. A corduroy skirt and a military-style raincoat completed her outfit.

Kohn made the introduction, one hand touching the girl's shoulder.

"Scott Hamilton, Gunilla von Mayenfels."

Her fingers rested briefly in Hamilton's; her voice was deep and modulated and without trace of accent.

"How do you do, Mr. Hamilton."

He smiled, trying to guess her age. The mesh of fine lines at the corners of her eyes could come from exposure to the sun. He gave her thirty at the outside. She'd probably look the same at forty. There was a touch of class about her that would save her from things like these terrible clothes and his own curiosity. Kohn wheeled an armchair at Hamilton and sat down facing them.

"Would anyone like a drink before we start?"

The girl's eyes barely drooped but the refusal was apparent. She was sitting with her skirt hiked-up, showing an inch of bare brown thigh. She was either unaware of it or indifferent. Hamilton shook his head. He was here to be told what he had to steal and this woman was part of the deal. He was aware of a totally new sensation, neither fear nor excitement but somewhere between the two.

Something like it seemed to be affecting the other pair. Kohn shaved his fleshy nose with his finger, his eyes watchful.

"Gunilla has to return to Lisbon this afternoon so we don't have much time. I think the best thing to do is take events in their proper sequence."

The girl held her cigarette like a pen, with two fingers and a thumb. She blew smoke in Hamilton's direction.

"Whichever way you want. We already agreed on this."

Kohn pointed at the simply framed portrait on the grand piano. The likeness was of a man wearing pince-nez and an old-fashioned stand-up collar. "My father," he said. The resemblance about the nose and eyes was unmistakable. Kohn felt in his jacket pocket and held up a dog-eared snapshot that had seen the inside of too many drawers. There was nothing on it but a numbered cement post sticking up out of unkempt grass. Kohn put it back in his pocket.

"That is a picture of my father's grave somewhere in Saxony. We don't know the exact location."

Hamilton propped a Disque-Bleu between his lips. The opening had the marks of the Wicked Nazi story and he wondered what it had to do with larceny. The girl's fine-boned impassive face gave him no help. Anyone else would have done herself an injury holding a cigarette like that.

Kohn's massive head brooded for a few seconds. "My father was a jeweler in business in Berlin. We had an apartment over the store on Kurfürstendam but our home was in the Spreewald. My father planted trees at the weekends and gave money to charity regardless of creed." He looked up at Hamilton.

The Canadian nodded, feeling it was the least he could do. The girl's position hadn't changed. She was twisting the signet ring on her left hand. That and a simple watch on a strap was the only jewelry she wore. Kohn continued.

"Jade was my father's mistress, his real love. My mother used to make jokes about it. I can remember as a child being told to close my eyes and try to tell the color of some piece my father had brought back from a buying trip. He claimed that a true lover of jade had eyes in his fingertips. Anyway, in nineteen thirty-three, three articles were auctioned in Kastner's in Berlin, jade statuettes carved in the form of dragons for a Ming Dynasty emperor in the late fifteenth century. The dragons were identical except for their eyes. One had emeralds, another rubies, the third sapphires. My father bought them and established their history. They represented three of the five Confucian virtues. The rubies stood for justice, the sapphires for reverence, the emeralds for sincerity. This left two dragons missing, one with pearl eyes for wisdom and the other, diamonds for love."

He heaved himself up, went to a lacquered cabinet and came back with a glass of mineral water. He patted his lips with his handkerchief.

"My father was the only man in Berlin who understood the significance of the dragons as well as their value. He finally tracked down the two missing pieces and bought them. That was in Warsaw in nineteen thirty-five. The collection was finally complete, the crowning work of his life. He called it the Spreewald Collection. He said that the colors reminded him of the trees and the water."

He cleared his throat and sat, sipping the water. The painted porcelain clock ticked away. Hamilton lit a fresh cigarette. Kohn spoke with a kind of bitter wonder.

"My father was a German before a Jew. He loved his country. When the Nazis came to power we stayed and lived for three years, free and unmolested. My father always said Hitler was a maniac. He believed that one day we would wake to hear news of his confinement in a mental asylum. Then in July, nineteen thirty-eight, the Gestapo arrived at the store. They sealed the safes, sequestered my father's bank accounts and took him away with them. We never saw him again, dead or alive. There was a rumor afterward that the raid had been on Goering's order, that the Spreewald Collection had gone to Karinhalle. I don't know, but this much is certain, from that day to this not a single piece of it has come to light."

"What's it worth?" asked Hamilton. "Assuming it still exists."

Kohn juggled his fat hands. "My father insured it for two hundred thousand pounds forty years ago. You can multiply that figure by ten. The truth is that these pieces are living history, Scott. It's impossible to assess their value."

The face of the clock caught the pale light from the window. Hamilton leaned forward, offering the girl a match as Kohn's eyes rested on her speculatively.

"I work with jewelers all over the world and my interest in the Spreewald Collection is well known. Gunilla came to see me two months ago, sent by a colleague in Lisbon. Tell Mr. Hamilton about it, Gunilla."

She nodded slowly, eyebrows like camel-hair brushes meeting as she frowned. "I'd gone to him for advice. First I have to explain. I was born in Lisbon where my father was First Secretary to the German Embassy. My mother died in childbirth and my aunt came to keep house for us. She wasn't really my aunt but my father's cousin. On the sixth of May, nineteen forty-five, a courier arrived from Berlin with a sealed bag. It was delivered to my father who was the embassy security officer and he locked it away in the strong room. The next day a signal came from the Foreign Ministry that Germany was on the point of surrender. The embassy staff started burning the code books and secret papers. That night my father disappeared. No one ever saw him again."

Hamilton shrugged. "Don't tell me! The bag went too. Well, it was the end of another empire. Men do strange things."

Her eyes darkened with intensity. The look she gave him was one of pure hatred.

"My father was an honorable man, Mr. Hamilton."

Kohn clucked into action, bringing order to the nest. "Tell him the rest, then he'll understand."

She made a small sound high in her nose and continued. "I was eleven months old when my father vanished. But I still know the sort of man he was."

Hamilton held up his hand in apology but he sensed that the damage had been done.

"About this bag that disappeared. You mean that Kohn's jade was inside it?"

Kohn's tone was cool. "You find that hard to believe?"

Hamilton turned with a smile. "Look, I don't want two of you at my throat; I'm groping. No, I don't find it hard to believe. In fact I'd say it was logical in the circumstances."

Kohn shook his head. "We have to be frank and we

have to be friends. I know you both and we're in this together. Now please, Scott. Let her talk and don't interrupt."

Gunilla lifted a gingham-clad shoulder. "We were left with a very small house and little money. Years later a lawyer in Lisbon contacted my aunt and said I was going to boarding school. The fees would be paid by a man called Baron Szily, a millionaire recluse who lived in the mountains behind Estoril. The lawyer said that Szily had been a friend of my father's. But he warned Tante Taube that any attempt to contact Szily would mean that the payments would stop. Years went by. I finished school at Heathfield in England and came back to Lisbon. Tante Taube had died by this time. I had a couple of jobs and then last September Szily's secretary got in touch with me."

She broke off to light another smoke. "Am I allowed to ask why?" said Hamilton. "I mean why get in touch with you?"

Her eyes fastened on his. He sensed that she still hadn't forgiven him.

"Curiosity perhaps. After all, he'd paid for my schooling but he'd never seen me. The German community in Portugal was small after the war. People said that my father had taken the jade to South America. I never heard of Szily saying anything in contradiction. The point was that he was giving me a job. He has this estate called Penha Longa with a private museum. The old catalogue was out of date and in German. He wanted me to make a new one in German and Portuguese. He was charming to me but he talked as if I were supposed to know that my father was dead. He wouldn't discuss it further but then that is the way he was. You accepted his terms or you went. The salary he offered me was four times as much as I had been getting. He said it didn't matter how long I took as long as the descriptions were accurate. I worked in the library. No one but Baron Szily was allowed in the museum itself, he even cleaned it out. Every morning he'd give me some things, paintings, a carving, an icon. There was no way of telling what he would choose. Then at night he'd collect the articles and return them to the museum."

Hamilton leaned back and joined his fingertips. "And this is the place you want me to burgle?"

Kohn nodded ponderously. "Apparently the museum has a glass dome but no windows. The glass is specially toughened. Entrance is made through a steel door from the library. There are two hundred hectares of woods and garden, a private golf course and two Doberman dogs that run loose at night."

Hamilton's shoulders slipped lower on the red leather. "Money's getting tougher to earn. Does anyone know how this steel door operates?"

"It rolls," the girl said calmly. She seemed quite unimpressed by his function and expertise. "The key never leaves Szily's person but the maid who takes his breakfast up says he sleeps with the key beneath his pillow. It's a little key with notches around the barrel and levers on both sides."

"I know what this sort of key looks like," he said.

"I'm sure you do," she said caustically. "Mr. Kohn might not be quite as expert."

Hamilton grinned despite himself. "Do we *have* to have her?" he demanded.

Kohn's face was serious. "I'm afraid we do, Scott."

Hamilton lifted a lazy hand. "Then it looks as if we're stuck with one another. Tell me about the house itself. How many people actually sleep there besides Szily?"

She scratched the tip of her nose delicately without taking her eyes off Hamilton.

"Nobody. He is the only one. The secretary has a flat over the garage. The servants' quarters are three hundred meters from the big house and the guesthouse is seldom used."

He tried to get a mental picture of the place but failed. "Let's get back to this jade. What makes you think that Szily has it locked away in his museum?"

She spread her palms expressively. "It was late one afternoon and Szily was on the driving range. I was going through some old Polish prints he had given to me to catalogue and I came across this colored Polaroid picture. You know, the cameras that develop their own films? It was a picture showing five small jade dragons with jeweled eyes. The important thing to me was that there was a date on the side of the picture, the date it had been taken. December 14, 1969. I just stood there and gaped at it when Szily walked in. I hadn't heard him. I thought for one moment he was going to hit me. Then he snatched the picture out of my hand and ordered me out of the house. There was no explanation, nothing. The following day a check for forty thousand escudos arrived in the mail, a month's salary. And that was the real beginning of the story."

"And you didn't go to the police?" He made it sound the most natural thing in the world.

Her tone was as sharp as lemon. "I take it you haven't lived in a country like Portugal. Szily leaves Penha Longa once a year to lunch with the President of the Republic. He has no children. Everything he owns will go to the State. You don't complain to the police about a man like that. I have to go," she said suddenly, turning to Kohn.

He took her arm protectively. "Happier than when you came, no?"

She gave him her fleeting smile. "I'll tell you that in Lisbon."

Kohn took her down to the street and a cab. He was back again in a couple of minutes, smoothing the crest of white hair at the back of his head.

"What do you think?" he asked flatly.

Hamilton's eyes were curious. "About what?"

Kohn sat down heavily. "I wanted you to hear all that at first hand. You're the expert."

"Well, I'd say she's on the level. She's up tighter than a drum and highly suspicious of me but she's on the level."

"I think so, too," said Kohn. "You've got to try to understand this girl, Scott. She's a very determined young lady obsessed with the idea of clearing her father's name. Nothing else in life really matters to her."

Hamilton took a turn to the window and stood looking down into the garden. A robin had bullied its way onto the coconut and swung there menacingly. He spoke with his back to his host.

"There's something I ought to explain. There's been a story going around for years that I brought disgrace on my family. The truth is that my mother skipped town to find me under a gooseberry bush in the Toronto General Hospital. My father's name is pure guesswork." He turned on his heel, smiling.

Kohn's cheeks filled and deflated. "I'm sorry."

Hamilton continued to smile. "Don't be sorry. The thing is that I find it hard to relate to a lot of what I've been hearing here. I mean the genuflections and all in the direction of one's parents. It doesn't mean beans to me, but I find it a strange situation, you two people worrying about your fathers' images. One a Jew, the other a Nazi."

Kohn pressed his weight into the red Moroccan leather. "It worried me at first but no longer. Can I have a quarrel with someone more troubled in spirit than I am? Look, I'm a Jew, as you say. And because of it there are organizations that I support. Worldwide organizations with excellent sources of information." He rubbed his hands together in a rare flash of clowning. "The wily Hebes, you know? Anyway, when Gunilla came here the first time, I naturally made some inquiries about her family. Would you like to hear the results?"

Hamilton came back to his seat. "Why not. I'm just walking around with my eyes shut, anyway."

Leather creaked as Kohn's weight spilled forward. "I'd rather you say nothing to her about it."

"You make the rules," said Hamilton.

"I wish I did," said Kohn. "Klaus-Dieter von Mayenfels, eldest son of respected Rhenish parents, a Hitler Jugend standard-bearer before passing the Foreign Office examinations. People like that were chosen very carefully. The future of Germany was meant to be in their hands. It is inconceivable that Mayenfels could have been a traitor. We know for sure now that the Spreewald Collection reached Lisbon on May sixth, nineteen forty-five, on its way to Buenos Aires. I was told that only two days ago. Remember that Germany was on the point of surrender. Mayenfels was security officer. It would have been his decision what to do with my father's jade. A courier might defect or be arrested by the Allied Forces but here's Szily, a known party-sympathizer and virtually sacrosanct. What better than to entrust the valuables to him? I believe that Mayenfels did just that and that Szily killed him afterward."

"Why?"

"I've had some inquiries made about Szily too. He's a fanatical collector, a lover of beautiful things and a man who has always made his own laws. He closed down three coal mines in Silesia rather than give in to the government over safety regulations. I believe that a man like that is capable of going to extremes."

"Such as *killing?* Come on, now, Philip. That sounds kind of heavy to me."

Kohn moved his head obstinately. "Mayenfels would have taken precautions not to be seen going to Szily's place. A single shot late at night. The body buried somewhere in the woods by Szily's retainers. I find that easy to believe."

Hamilton worried the statement to its logical conclusion. "I'm not so sure I like the way that your mind is working. Or whether we're talking about the same thing as last night. OK. This collection was your father's lifework, I'll buy that. And maybe Szily wanted it. I'll buy that one too. But you said he's a millionaire. One question. How many millionaires did you ever hear of who shoot people and bury the bodies in woods?"

Kohn's mouth drooped. "That part of it is no more than surmised, I'll agree. But the rest is certain. Szily has the Spreewald Collection. Now I know it's not going to be easy, Scott. That's why there'll be another man working with you."

Hamilton stayed the match halfway to his mouth. "Another *man!* Who?"

Kohn's voice slid into a persuasive register. "Someone reliable. Don't worry about it."

Hamilton touched the flame to the French cigarette. "Don't *tell* me don't worry; I get neurotic. I never worked with anyone else in my life. Who is this guy anyway?"

Kohn looked across at the painted clock, his voice casual now as though the matter under discussion was of little importance.

"He's a private inquiry agent living in Paris. He's reliable and vouched for by an old friend. He'll do exactly what you tell him and you need all the help you can get. You'll see. You'll meet him in Lisbon. How long do you think it would take, Scott? I mean, once you're there."

"The sooner the better," said Hamilton. The tea and toast had long been digested and his stomach was rumbling. More than anything else he wanted to soak in a bath and think. He stuffed the pack of French cigarettes back in his pocket. "I'll need to see the place first, get the feel of things. Set it up with the girl for whenever you like. When do you want me to leave?"

"Tomorrow morning." Kohn passed over a flight ticket.

There were five ten-pound notes tucked inside the folder. "Eleven forty-five from Heathrow. I've booked a room for you at the Westmoreland Hotel near the terminal. In Lisbon you're at the Carlton. You'll find the details on the paper. We'll meet tomorrow and I'll give you half your money, the rest on completion. Is that fair, I mean normal?"

Kohn looked so earnest that Hamilton was hard pushed not to laugh outright. The mixture of banal chat and suave Greenstreet villainy was difficult to take.

"It's fair, Philip," he said. "I think I'll be running along. There are things I have to do. I'd like you to tell me something before I go. What made you so sure of yourself? Getting that girl here, booking hotels and the rest. Suppose I'd told you no go?"

Kohn lumbered up, sniffing at the rose in his buttonhole before he replied.

"Then I would have lost too much for the rest to matter."

Hamilton scratched through his long graying hair. "You're a liar but I like it. You'd have gone ahead with the guy from Paris, right?"

"I honestly don't know," Kohn said soberly. "It never entered my mind that you wouldn't help me."

Hamilton put out his hand. Neither a great rogue nor a great innocent, Kohn was suddenly nothing more than a tired old man.

"Everything's going to be OK."

Kohn's voice had the ring of faith.

"I believe so. Right is on our side and that counts."

Hamilton released his fingers. It was no good pointing

out that a whole lot of guys had been carted off to jail saying precisely the same thing.

"Don't bother seeing me out. I'll ring you this evening."

The woman downstairs had shifted her chair so that she faced the hallway door. She lowered her book deliberately as Hamilton made for the steps to the street. She was younger than he had thought with dark Slavic eyes. He smiled politely but she just sat there looking at him, tapping her teeth with the end of her fingernail. Fine, thought Hamilton, that would be one woman who wouldn't be walking through the edges of his dreams. He strolled west, his eyes open for a cab. He was through with buses.

The Westmoreland was a fifteen-story hotel built in the slab-fronted fashion of the seventies with a Jamaican doorman and a chrome-and-glass revolving entrance. A closed-circuit scanner followed Hamilton through the Byzantine lobby to the reception desk. He checked in and an Irish bellhop carried his bag upstairs. The room was not much larger than the cell he had recently vacated. The single bed faced a window overlooking the back of Gloucester Road subway station. There was a DanArt clothes-closet, a coin-operated television set and a drinks dispenser. The small writing desk offered a copy of *What's On* and a ball-point pen inscribed with the compliments of the management. The bathroom was clinically clean, the lavatory seat was guaranteed sterile and the towels smelled of chloride. He hung a sign on the outside of the door and locked himself in. By and large his quarters were about as inviting as a dentist's waiting room. He unpacked his bag, changed into his one pair of silk pajamas and lay down on top of the bed. His stomach was still rumbling. After a while he picked up the phone and asked for room service. Minutes later someone tapped softly on the door. He signed the check, tipped the Cypriot waiter and turned the key again. The food under the nickel-silver covers was terrible, the steak overcooked, the celery tasting of mouthwash. He ate it standing, popped a can of beer from the drinks-dispenser and lay down again.

OK, now it was time to see what exactly he had gotten himself into. To examine his conscience, as the Brothers had been used to putting it. So, compose the thought and examine the conscience. If you took Kohn's caper apart and examined the pieces separately, each had a genuine ring. On the face of things this was a straightforward job with the odds more or less in his favor. He was as good an operator as he ever had been, maybe a little better now that he knew what the inside of a jail looked like. He was thirty-eight years old, no ties, no responsibilities. And three thousand pounds represented a lot of mileage. Once he'd earned it he could sit in the sunshine somewhere and think about his next move. Or maybe he'd just sit. They said that certain things in life were preordained. If that was true, then planning how to avoid them was just frosting your balls.

He yawned, stretched and checked his watch. It was almost two o'clock. He pulled out the race sheet in his newspaper. There was steeplechasing on the tube. He fed the set a couple of coins and adjusted the color. The names of the horses were unfamiliar and he picked three losers in a row before killing the picture. Then he dozed for a while on a beach with banana palms. The light outside was fading when he fully woke. He lifted the phone from the hook and asked for a number. The remembered voice was as husky as ever.

"Hi," he said. "It's Scott Hamilton."

There was a gasp. "Jesus Christ!"

"Come on now," he said. "You can do better than that. That's no kind of welcome."

He leaned back on the pillows, holding the phone with his chin as he lit a smoke.

Paula Davey had herself under control again. "You took my breath away, you beast! Where are you anyway?"

"In London." He blew a stream of smoke at the window. "How's Tim?"

She hesitated for a fraction of a second. "He's fine. He's got this new thing about Swedish *au pairs* but he's fine. When did you . . . "

"This morning," he said easily. "I'm flying out in the morning. I thought it would be nice to see you people again before I went. You know?"

"But *of course,* darling," she hurried. "And why didn't you write to us?"

He scored her high for a frontal attack. "I did. As a matter of fact I wrote twice. The letters were returned."

"We never had them," she insisted stoutly. "Not a single word. We wondered why. Tim thought that it might have been because of Mariga. You know, that you blamed us for what happened."

He could see himself in the bathroom mirror and winked at his reflection. Paula Davey's voice sounded with tinny insistence.

"Scott? Are you there?"

"I'm here," he answered. "Blame you for what? The thirty-eight hundred pounds she stole or that golf bum?"

Her tone stumbled but recovered quickly. "Nobody had the slightest idea what she was up to till the very last minute. Not that there was anything that we could have done about it. You know Mariga."

"The hell with Mariga," he said deliberately. "She's a rip-off as far as I'm concerned. I'm calling a couple of old friends I've not seen for years."

"Of course," she gushed. "Come as soon as you like. How about six-thirty? The girl doesn't come on duty till eight and we'll have the place to ourselves."

He put the phone down as she mashed a couple of kisses into the mouthpiece. Nothing had changed in that direction. She was still serving up the schmaltz. But he'd shaken her and was glad of it. He'd lain awake too many nights thinking about the Daveys to let them off the hook completely. Tim and Paula, his very good friends. They'd hammered it into his head as often as he had paid their bar bills. And one of them, if not both, had blown the whistle on him. Cain had as good as admitted it. It was Tim who had introduced him to Mariga Fitzpatrick. *A model but a really super chick and completely unspoiled.*

The sky outside was completely dark, with neon signs flashing on and off beyond the subway station. He drew the curtains, ran himself a bath and used his razor for the second time that day. The smell of mothballs had evaporated from his suit. The strip of light over the mirror tinged his hair with yellow, making his face lined and haggard. What could you expect after three years in the pokey? Thank God that his teeth had held up. He knotted his tie, collected his leather coat and rode the elevator down to a lobby crowded with French tourists. He walked past them out into the chilly darkness. It was like being born again. The feeling of freedom was absolute. There were no screws slamming doors and doing their snide numbers, no more days to divide into hours. He turned right on Gloucester Road. The blinking signs he had seen from his window advertised take-away pizza, lightning shoe repairs and while-you-wait cleaning. The temperature had dropped five degrees since morning. Cold peaked the faces of the Asians and Africans clustered in the doorway of the Berlitz Schools of Languages. The homecoming crowds were still streaming out of the subway, grabbing their groceries and heading for any one of the ten thousand flats and bed-sitters in the neighborhood. The City and West End sucked these people in every morning and spewed them out again at night.

All the cabs he saw were being occupied. The eastbound train he boarded was practically empty. He surfaced at Green Park and hurried north to Shepherd Market. The hookers were already out, soliciting from doorways along the narrow streets and passages. Restaurants offered the delights of transvestite singers, belly dancers, and there were the staider comforts of corner pubs. Doorways promised warmth and shelter. He brushed past a black teen-age whore in a blond wig. The café window behind her was crowded with morose-faced men guarding their food with their elbows. The small house he was looking for was sandwiched between a bookstore and a place that sold travel goods. The front windows were screened with heavy curtains. A lavender-colored sign on the door read

KUBLA KHAN CLUB MEMBERS ONLY

He put his hand on the door with an apprehension of being about to do the wrong thing one more time in his life. The last time he'd put foot in this house had been with Mariga. She'd been working that day and he'd picked her up at the studio. They'd come on to the club for a drink. Minutes later the law had arrived. He'd been relaxed enough at first. Cain and his buddy had played it very cool, calling him out of the bar onto the landing. His first thought was that he was about to be questioned over some traffic offense. Then one had grabbed his arms while the other went through his pockets. There was no chance for him to get rid of the safe-deposit key. They'd marched him out to the waiting police car and held him overnight in Chelsea Police Station. Events speeded up in the morning. By ten o'clock his apartment had been turned upside down. Another half-hour and he found himself in the charge room confronted with the diamond-and-emerald necklace they had found in the safe-deposit box. He'd been hanging on to it for almost four months, a crazy thing to have done, yet at the time it had seemed reasonable.

He had landed in England intent on becoming a burglar. He'd tried and failed about everything else. Luck had been with him from the start, the sort of luck he'd never had before. He rented a small office in Victoria, filled some files and a showcase with job lots of coins and commemorative medals and stuck a sign on the door. Then he'd gone to work, choosing his hits carefully, cataloguing women's jewelry at restaurant tables, following them on the street, reading about them in gossip columns. He searched electoral lists, worked as a temporary postman, gathered material for opinion polls, posed as an estate agent. At the end of five years he'd racked up thirty profitable scores without as much as a question asked. He taught himself how to break up jewelry, operating behind locked doors in his office. Every three months or so, he made a trip to Zurich or Amsterdam selling loose stones for hard cash. He never bothered with gold or platinum, dropping these metals in the river. His pose as a successful coin-dealer justified his frequent absences from the country and the considerable sums of money he was spending. The people he knew, the management of the block he lived in, appeared to accept his cover completely. He never made a confidant, not even of Mariga. But the Daveys had caught on somewhere along the line. A whole group of oddballs used their club, including a couple of aristocratic hash-dealers. Tim Davey was into a couple of heavy scenes which must have been his reason for blowing the whistle.

Hamilton turned the handle and stepped into the tiny entrance hall. A row of empty coat hangers extended behind an empty desk. A bowl of yellow freesias in front of the wall-heater scented the air. He climbed the stairs to the second story and rattled his knuckles on a door. The Daveys lived up on the third. The door swung wide on a spindly blond man with a Mexican villain's mustache. He was wearing Levi's stuffed into tooled-leather boots and a black roll-neck sweater accentuated the narrowness of his shoulders. He threw his arms wide, a rubbery smile drawing his mustache up with it.

"Scott, you old bugger!"

Hamilton closed the door carefully. The room looked much the same as it had on the night of his arrest. Pink bracket-lamps, flocked wallpaper, crimson velvet curtains and chair cushions. Paula Davey reached out from behind the bar, shaking back her long red hair. He went through the motions of touching her cheek with his mouth and shook his head.

"I swear to God you don't look a day older, Paula!"

Overripe breasts bulged under a Jean Muir dress and her eyes and mouth had been subjected to a heavy paint job.

"You're a lovely man, Scott Hamilton," she said fulsomely.

He closed an eye in acknowledgment. The courtesies weren't going to last that long. She was still going with the batting-eyelashes number and the mouth falling open like a fish. She spun the bottle of Dom Perigot in the ice bucket. Her magenta-tinted nails were the same shade as her lips. Tim Davey lounged across and arranged himself on a barstool. His wife filled three tulip-shaped glasses and used a whisky on Hamilton's.

"No bubbles. Everything the way you like it, Scott, darling."

He tried the wine. It was cold and it was good. He raised his glass. "Cheers!" He kept his tone quiet and conversational. "To the greatest pair of backstabbers in the business!"

The smile on Paula Davey's face was wiped clean as if with a sponge. A look of wary expectation replaced it.

"What's that supposed to mean?"

He cocked his head at her. "Why did you people turn me in? What exactly did Cain have to offer?"

Paula Davey backed off a couple of paces, her mouth as mean as a hyena's.

"Don't pay any attention to that smile, Tim. I warned you — he's here to make trouble."

"Is that right? Don't you trust us?" demanded Davey.

Hamilton shook his head. "I wouldn't like to go to sleep with my finger in your mouth."

"Get him out of here," Paula Davey said in a hard penetrating voice.

Her husband's hand silenced her. "It's not the way you think, Scott. I can explain. You've got Mariga to thank for your trouble. Look, why not let Paula roll us some joints and we'll talk this thing through to the end."

Hamilton dangled the wine bottle between his thumb and forefinger. "Relax. There isn't going to *be* any trouble. You people could never get your heads right about me, could you?"

Paula Davey's expression was frankly malevolent. "It wasn't Mariga, it was me."

Hamilton lowered the bottle carefully. "Well, at least we've got that much out into the open."

Davey interposed his spiderlike body between them. "Let it go, Scott," he pleaded. "It's better, I promise you. Just let it go."

His wife's eyes glittered balefully. She was sweating and scared but indomitable.

"I want him out of here, Tim. Out of this bar. If he doesn't go I'm going to call the police."

The taste of the wine was sour in Hamilton's mouth. The whole exercise had suddenly gone flat.

"Not you, Paula. Not this time, you won't. You can't afford it."

The edginess seemed to be catching. Davey's hand was shaking. "I'm sorry it had to end this way, Scott."

His wife's face was furious. "Cry on each other's shoulders, why don't you? Let me tell you something, Scott Hamilton. I never liked you from the beginning, the big spender with the big phony smile. The only person you ever gave a damn about is yourself and Mariga's well shot of you. Take that with you when you fly out tomorrow and think about it!"

"You're wonderful," said Hamilton, picking up his overcoat. "All the finesse of a fishwife. OK, I'm going now but let me leave you with a word of sound advice. You people ever run across me again, keep a very low profile."

By the time he reached the park end of Curzon Street, his pulse rate was back to normal. He ate a bowl of chili in a restaurant on King's Road. It might seem that he had achieved nothing. What Paula Davey had done to him would have earned her a hit in the head in some circumstances. But violence, other than as a kid on the hockey rink, had never been his bag. The truth was that there were things a man had to do that made no sense except to himself. He drank two cold beers and paid his check. The temperature outside had dipped another couple of degrees. He pulled his belt tighter, turned his collar up and walked briskly west. This next call was going to be a lot harder to handle. He had to ask a favor from a man whose lack of charity was notorious. Albie Dean had landed in England shortly after the war, an ex-jockey barred for life wherever there was organized horse racing. Delicate artistry with a file combined with a larcenous heart had turned him into just about the best maker of false keys in the country. He sold his skills to a chosen few, shuddered at the mention of the law and pleaded poverty at the first hint of a touch.

Hamilton turned left toward the barrackslike apartment buildings that extended south as far as the river. Each had its own grim waste of asphalt marked off as volleyball court and playground. The street lamps were protected by wire cages. Any fixture not bolted down had been damaged or removed. The walls of the entrance hall were decorated with primitive *graffiti*. The elevators were permanently out of order. Hamilton climbed ten bare concrete floors to the top, followed by the rich aroma of frying onions. A couple of doors faced one another. He rapped hard on the one on the right. A crack of light showed at the bottom of the door but there was no answer. He bent down and lifted the mail flap. A piece of felt inside prevented him from seeing through.

"It's me, Albie," he shouted. "Scott Hamilton."

The spring-loaded flap descended, just missing his fingertips. The voice from inside was unmistakably Australian.

"What the hell do you want?"

Hamilton straightened up, bringing his mouth to the chink of the door.

"I want you to open up, Albie. It's important."

A chain rattled and keys turned. Albie Dean was short, bald and bandy-legged with suspicious eyes in a crumpled face. He wore a tea-stained flannel shirt, cord trousers that were belted under a bulge of belly and two-tone brown shoes. He let Hamilton in, eyeing him with a sour grin.

"If it isn't Raffles himself! And when pray did they turn *you* loose?"

"This morning." Hamilton started to wheedle his way forward. "Look, it's cold, Albie. You're not going to keep me standing out here, are you? Not after all that we've been to one another?"

Dean backed off, shaking his head against the blandishment. "You've got some nerve coming here. I lent you three skeleton keys, the genuine articles from Chubb. With them keys a man could have gone through the Bank of England like a hot fly through butter. And what happens, the fucking law picks them out of your safe-deposit box! And you have the nerve to walk in here, grinning all over your face like Prince Charming."

"You've got a foul mouth," Hamilton said sadly.

Dean blinked, leaning both hands on the wall and blocking the passageway.

"You cocky bastard! What would you have *been* without the twirls I made for you? Nothing!"

"A bare-faced exaggeration," Hamilton said cheerfully. "Think of all the money you earned from me."

Dean seemed to extract some satisfaction from the thought. "I must have made fifteen sets for you over the years. All that crap about dropping them down the drain when you'd used them. Insurance, you said, and what happens — you get done with the gear like some boy burglar and lose three keys I can't replace."

"Can't we go in?" pleaded Hamilton. He could see the fire burning in the comfortable room at the end of the passageway. "Come on, Albie, what do you say?"

Dean moved his arms from the walls. "I suppose," he said grudgingly. "Listening to you can't be worse than the television programs they're putting out."

The focal point in the living room was a giant color set with all the refinements. The table was pulled to one side to allow unimpeded vision. An old-fashioned dresser packed the end wall. Dean had been eating from the frying pan. A knife and fork were side by side with a sausage embalmed in cold grease. On the mantel were pictures of Dean crouched on a horse's neck passing a winning post. He toed a chair in Hamilton's direction.

"OK, Hamilton, let's have it. If your problem's money I've got none." He opened the dresser and poured Scotch into two cups. "And all the glasses are broke. Cheers."

"Cheers," answered Hamilton. The cup bore the clear impression of Albie's thumbprint. "I'll lay it on you, Albie. I need a favor."

Dean started visibly. "Then you come to the wrong place, mate. I'm no particular friend of yours. Besides that, I'm fifty-five years old, and I've got heartburn. There's nothing there for you."

Hamilton put his cup on the dresser. Dean was watching his every movement with narrowed eyes.

"You earned good money with me, Albie," Hamilton

said, leaning against the mantel. "No one else ever gave you a bonus. You told me that yourself."

"That was years ago," Dean answered, stretching his bandy legs. "You lost my keys since then."

"That's what I want," said Hamilton, looking down and winking. "The number one outfit and I need it now, tonight. I'm off in the morning."

"Off?" repeated Dean. "Off where?"

"Portugal," said Hamilton.

Dean's hand shot out. "And you come to *me* for keys?"

"Listen to me," argued Hamilton. "I'll give you two hundred quid and a guarantee that they won't be used in this country. Fifty pounds down, and the rest in a week, and remember, I never welshed on you."

"Nobody did," Dean said acidly. "It's a funny thing. I always had an idea that I'd seen the last of you. I thought you'd turn the game in when you came out, write a book or marry some old bag for her money. I told you, you're out of touch. Things are different all round. Old Bill slips about very lively these days."

"I'm glad to hear it," said Hamilton. "I like to see a keen police force. It keeps the rest of us on our toes."

"You're a cocky bastard," said Dean. "What's this about keys and Portugal?"

Hamilton scratched a match on the side of the box. Dean didn't smoke and there were no ashtrays. He used the dirty cup.

"It's a job. A country house where the people are burglar-conscious. I want you to dig down under the floorboards and get me what I need. The money may not be much but it's in a good cause."

Dean stared at him with reluctant admiration. The smell of cooking from downstairs had crept into the apartment together with the noise of a baby crying.

"Do you know why I'm going to help you?" Dean said at length. "It isn't the money and for my part you can stick the keys up the King of Portugal's ass when you've done with them."

Hamilton turned his hand over this way and that. "It's because I restore your faith in human nature."

"You're crazy, that's why," Dean said flatly. "I just don't have the right to refuse you. A few hours out of the nick and taking on some job in Portugal! Don't tell me no more. I don't want to hear it. Give me the fifty." He stuck out his dirty palm.

Hamilton counted out five tens. "I'll ask Saint Jude to intercede for you."

Dean belched and tapped the side of his head. "You're unbalanced, mate. A menace to society, that's what you are. Now stay there. I don't want the likes of you in my bedroom."

He was back in a few minutes, bouncing a small suede satchel in his hand.

"The best in the country, without any question."

"What are you, some kind of a wise guy? Stop playing Hamlet and let me see!"

There were two rings of beautifully tooled skeleton keys, ten keys to each ring, varying in size and pattern. There was a set of picklocks looking like flanged knitting needles, a tiny wood-drill powered by a battery in the handle, surgical forceps to grip and turn a key in the lock. A small roll of piano wire and a penlight completed the outfit. Hamilton stuffed the satchel into his overcoat pocket.

"Thanks."

"I don't know why I'm so generous," said Dean. "I must be slipping."

"You're about as generous as a blackjack dealer. Who were these made for anyway?"

Dean scratched the end of his flattened nose. "Some college boy who knew it all like you. Ended up by falling off a roof."

Hamilton winced. "And killed himself?"

"Worse," said Dean. "He broke both legs and stayed there for the law to pick him up. He's doing twelve on the Island. Never did collect his keys."

It required an effort for Hamilton to wipe the image from his mind.

"One other thing before I go. What do people do with dogs?"

Dean scowled. "They cover the streets with dogshit, why? Don't tell me you've got a dog!"

"I'm talking about guard dogs," said Hamilton. "I always ran a mile from them."

"You did well," Dean said sourly. His feelings on the subject were obviously strong. "You mean you got *them* to deal with too? Then you really are sick in the head."

"I know," said Hamilton. "How about that Larry Maloney? He was always supposed to be spooking dogs and you did business with him. He must have told you how he did it."

"He barked," said Dean. He mellowed suddenly, either because of the fifty pounds or his role as Elder Statesman. "I'll tell you a story. Years ago there used to be a greyhound track back in Brisbane, the crookedest track in Australia. No one who went there figured to lose his money. They used to stop the electric hare, shoot the dogs up the ass with airgun pellets and this one night a geezer threw a cat out onto the track. Do you know what those bleedin' greyhounds did?"

Hamilton thought for a moment. Someone had lit a bonfire on the asphalt playground below. The flames were feet high, licking up into the night.

"Kept running, I guess. They're trained to chase the hare."

A look of sly satisfaction slid across Dean's face. "Wrong. That cat was soaked in aniseed. They chased the fucker clean up a flagpole and all bets were void. And *that's* what Maloney did with guard dogs, mate. He distracted their attention."

Hamilton patted Dean on the shoulder. "Thanks, Albie. You'll be hearing from me."

Dean nodded grimly. "I hope so, mate. You owe me money."

He shuffled down the passageway in front of Hamilton. The door was locked and the chain refastened before the Canadian had even started down the stairs. The library on Manresa Road was open. He went into the reference room and carried the heavy volume to a reading desk. The short article gave him all the information he needed. *A volatile oil with a strong aromatic taste and a powerful odor.* He checked the Home Office list of prescribed drugs. As far as he could see, aniseed could be bought freely. He put it to the test in the all-night drugstore on King's Road. A couple of minutes later he walked out with a four-ounce bottle in his pocket.

Sleep came with the suddenness of water at the foot of a twenty-meter-board dive.

II

Kohn put the receiver down very carefully. His voice sounded louder than usual.

"That was Kosky, the man Herschel sent from Paris. He's waiting for me in his hotel. He wants the money."

The woman sitting on the red leather couch glanced up from her embroidery. In private they always spoke German and she had never quite lost the Dresden accent of her childhood.

"Two thousand pounds — three to the other man. Are you sure it is wise?"

He unlocked a drawer in a lacquered table. The bills were in the briefcase, still banded with the bank's paper seals.

"He makes his own conditions. Herschel says he is to be trusted."

She nipped a thread with her teeth. She was wearing a black dress with a jade beetle pinned on one side. Her dark hair was braided and pulled forward over her left shoulder. Ten years had gone by since the shabbily dressed girl had climbed down from the Vienna express clutching a cheap fiber suitcase. Her journey to freedom had taken seven years with each stage marked by tragedy. First her mother, the distant cousin Kohn barely remembered, ravaged by a virus she had been too weak to resist. Then her father, the dreamer who had opened his veins in an Augsburg transit camp. And finally her husband, his back broken in some banal traffic accident, leaving her no more than Austrian nationality and the price of his funeral. Kohn had taken her to a quiet, softly lighted restaurant where the green Rhine flowed deep beneath the windows. She had eaten little, keeping her tilted Tartar eyes fixed on his face, refusing to talk about the past. He had brought her back to England to the house he had learned to call home. Within months she was part of it, warming his heart with her intelligence and charm. She had given him youth and love, scorning his feelings of guilt and doubt.

She frowned, shadowing skin the color of old ivory. "Herschel! A tea-dancer! A billiard-room Zionist! I'm sick of his very name."

He smiled indulgently. "An old friend, Milcah. We grew up together. From an old friend I have no secrets."

She made a sound of disgust. "From the secretary of the Maccabean League you have no secrets? I knew these people in Vienna, busybodies with their noses in strange places."

England had given her confidence but the memory of deceit and betrayal was still there close to the surface.

"Herschel knew my father," he assured her.

"Then why the sighs?" she challenged. "Is life so unbearable?"

He moved a hand uncertainly. "A feeling of apprehension. I suppose the truth is that I am too old for this sort of thing."

Her eyes were brilliant and piercing. "Of course you're too old! So give it up. Send them all packing, Kosky, the girl and your precious Hamilton. Learn to smoke a pipe like an Englishman and become a model of masterly inactivity!"

"Aiee!" he said and held up a hand. He tried to explain and floundered. "You don't understand."

She put her embroidery down very deliberately. "I understand very well. It was practical to talk of trust when you visited Hamilton once a week in prison. But now you are deeply involved and it's different. You tell yourself you are doing something unworthy and feel ashamed."

"I have to have Kosky," he said doggedly.

She drew him down on the couch beside her. "Now listen to me, darling. I watched your face the day that girl first came here with her story. I knew what it meant to you but I didn't approve. How could I?"

"Szily has the prize of my father's collection in his possession. Stolen. Is what I am doing wrong?"

Her eyes met his unwaveringly. "Should I answer you yes or no?"

"I must do it," he insisted.

"Of course you must," she said quickly. "We agreed on this and we agreed that your friend is a thief and a thief can be tempted. To make sure that he gives you what you pay him to take is not hypocritical, it's logical."

He lifted her palm to his lips. "What would I do without you, Milcah?"

"I wonder," she smiled. "You say this Kosky is a private detective?"

He shrugged. "An inquiry agent. He's a Brazilian so he speaks Portuguese."

She straightened his tie. "Then go to see him and put on your scarf. The air outside is bitterly cold. And drive carefully."

The Rolls-Royce Silver Shadow was three years old but gleaming and opulent. He buckled his seatbelt. Small prudences seemed to be part of his life, guarding him against folly, and here he was paying two thousand pounds to a stranger. His goal was a small hotel north of the park. He stopped outside the entrance and gave his keys to the doorman. The only people in the lobby were two Japanese businessmen with square-mouthed smiles and blue scalps gleaming through bristles of black hair. Kohn walked to the desk.

"Mr. Kosky, please. I am expected. My name is Leopold." The lie came with amazing ease.

The clerk nodded and snapped his fingers. "The boy will take you up, Mr. Leopold."

The elevator gate closed. Kohn stood looking into the crown of his homburg and thinking about Herschel. The Maccabean League was known to have helped in the search for Eichmann, and his old friend moved in strange circles. The bellhop slid the gate back and pointed down the silent corridor. The door Kohn knocked on was opened immediately. A thin man with a face like a ferret peered out with nervous red-rimmed eyes. He was in his late forties, wearing a speckled tweed suit and shoes with two-inch heels.

"Shalom!" he said.

It was a small room with a boxlike bed, a narrow clothes-closet and a small table. Kohn took the only chair. His dislike for Kosky was instant and complete.

"Don't you speak any English?"

Kosky perched on the bed, displaying clocked nylon socks that he seemed to admire.

"Yes, I do. I speak Portuguese, English, French and Hebrew. Bachelor of Science, São Paulo University."

Kohn threw the briefcase onto the bed. "You will find the amount correct but please count it. And keep the case."

Kosky's smile showed hoops of bone at the gumline, the mouth of a man who has suffered from scurvy.

"Herchel says you are a man of your word."

The tone stung as well as the words. "We have known one another for fifty years," Kohn said stiffly.

"The two things are not necessarily related," Kosky replied, scratching his hairy shank.

"Will you please count the money?" Kohn insisted.

Kosky riffed through the packaged bills and zipped the case up again.

"Alles in ordnung."

Kohn did his best to hide his dislike. Kosky's manner suggested an intimate knowledge of human frailty, of shameful secrets seen through keyholes and in the divorce court. The mere fact of being in the same room with him was an affront.

"Herschel has told you everything, given you the details?"

Kosky slipped the briefcase under the pillow. "Yes, but I'd like to hear from you. I make two rules in my business. I do not work on a contingency basis and I require complete frankness."

The room was close. Kohn loosened the cashmere scarf at his neck. He spoke with meticulous precision.

"You are being paid to break into a house with another man and retrieve certain articles. This other man is a professional burglar and you will follow his instructions. Your task is to ensure that these articles find their way back to me."

"The Spreewald Collection," Kosky said easily. "Your father was Max Kohn, the Berlin jeweler, no?"

Kohn looked up into knowing red-rimmed eyes. Blabbermouth Herschel.

"Do you think we might have the window open? I find it oppressively hot."

"I'm sorry," Kosky said smoothly. "I cannot stand drafts. This other man, the burglar. I understand that you're not too sure about him. You want me to watch him."

It was an ugly image and one that Kohn chose to forget. He spread his legs, bearing his weight down on his knees.

"You have an unfortunate way of putting things. Each of you has a job to do."

Kosky showed no sign of having been disciplined. "Will he be armed?"

"I doubt it," said Kohn. There was something unpleasant about the suggestion.

Kosky leaned back against the wall, yawning. "What time is it?"

Kohn looked at his watch. The platinum hands on a lapis lazuli face showed twenty after eleven.

"Your flight back to Paris is an early one?" he inquired politely.

"Fairly early." Kosky seemed to avoid specific statements. "I shall be in Lisbon by four o'clock. The Mondial Hotel, is that correct?"

"The Mondial." Kohn collected his homburg. "I shall telephone you there. My regards to Herschel if you see him before you leave."

Kosky opened the door and glanced both ways along the corridor. "Shalom!" he said and shut the door.

The lights in the lobby had been lowered except for the one at the desk. There was an air about the place, thought Kohn, that made it right for a meeting with someone like Kosky. He waited at the entrance as the doorman backed up the Rolls. He drove home through the park with head lamps scanning the bare trees and stretches of winter-brown turf. It was getting on for midnight and he couldn't rid his mind of a picture of Hamilton in a bar somewhere getting drunk. He left the Rolls under a lamp on Grosvenor Street and walked back to the house with the cold stiffening the hairs in his nostrils. The lights were still on in the sitting room. He double-locked the front door and switched on the burglar alarm. Most of his stock was in the vaults. He changed his display once a month, taking customers to the bank when necessary. The climb up the stairs left him short of breath. He had cut his cigars to five a day and there was nothing more he could do except retire. Dr. Laurie would approve of that, of course. Rest and relaxation. They'd turn him into some freak in a flannel suit hobbling about on the deck of a cruise ship. Only Milcah understood that without his work he'd be dead in a year.

She helped him out of his coat and hustled him into the warmth and comfort of the drawing room. The piano was open, the sheet music on top. She had been playing Brahms. He sank down gratefully. Chocolate was bubbling in a silver pot and there was a plate of the gingerbread he liked beside it. He rubbed his palms together briskly.

"You were right. It was cold outside."

She filled an earthenware bowl with chocolate and gave it to him. If he closed his eyes it was the house in the Spreewald, the lake through the woods frozen, his skates on the kitchen table, his mother and the maids clucking over his wet clothes. He opened his eyes again and Milcah was smiling down at him.

"Tomorrow you'll be in the sunshine. I have a good mind to come with you. There's no reason why Levisohn shouldn't take care of things here."

He wrapped his fingers around the bowl, disconsolate at the thought.

"A joke," she added quickly. "Forget about it."

He sipped the hot sweet brew to the end and wiped his mouth on the linen square.

"I am getting old, Milcah. Fear taps me on the shoulder far too often. I felt it tonight with Kosky."

He put the bowl back on the tray. The household chores were done by contract. A trio of silent, efficient men appeared, did their work and vanished. Milcah beckoned him across to the nest of scarlet leather. He sat down beside her.

"You are acting like an old woman," she told him gently. "Suspicious of everyone. First it was Hamilton, now it is Kosky. What, in God's name, is wrong with Kosky?"

He stared into his upturned palms as if the answer might be found there.

"I don't know. But I am sure of this. There is something evil about him."

She tugged at the back of his hair, forcing his head around. Her eyes were tender.

"What do you expect, angels with silver wings? These people are no more than a means to an end, Philip. That's all. A couple of days and they'll be gone from your life."

He was too tired to argue with her logic. "A means to an end," he agreed. For some reason or other the phrase was uglier in his mouth than in hers.

She dropped her sewing bag into the lacquered chest and smiled at him.

"Come on. I love you too much to let you sleep by yourself with your head filled with nonsense."

He listened to her footsteps going up the circular staircase. After a while he came to his feet and closed the piano. His father's portrait drew him like a magnet. When he was finally at peace with it he put the lights out and followed her up to bed.

III

THE PILOT extracted the last burst of power from the four jet engines. The final shudder was the signal for a free-for-all scramble for hand luggage. Hamilton was sitting up front, his overnight bag under the seat. He was first off the plane, bouncing down the gangway with a grin for the pert waiting hostess. The quality of the light outside was dazzling. It was as though his eyes had been peeled to fresh sensitivity. The airport buildings were sharply etched, the colors vibrant. He climbed into the bus and was promptly sealed in by an overweight Englishwoman wearing what looked like kitchen curtains. The pressure of her body expelled him like a cork when the doors opened again. He followed the white-gloved hostess into the arrival hall. Two desks ahead, men with wrap-around sunglasses sat inspecting passports. Hamilton took his place on the line, his stomach starting to waltz. It was a moment that he never relished. He'd have felt the same on a pilgrimage to Lourdes. He moved forward, doing his best to forget the satchel of burglar's tools in his pocket.

The plainclothesman whipped Hamilton's passport under a hundred-watt lamp.

"Canadian?" He managed to make it sound like a felony.

"That's right." A big smile for Brother John, the one with the ashplant.

"Where do you stay in Portugal?"

"In Lisbon," beamed Hamilton. "The Carlton Hotel."

"How long?"

The smile was beginning to make Hamilton's jaw ache. "I don't really know. A week, maybe more."

The cop thumbed through the passport for a blank space, rammed a stamp down and scribbled his initials. Hamilton tagged on to the crowd heading for the customs bays. An official in a baggy gray uniform chalked his bag and waved him on impatiently. The scene outside was lively after the gray restraint of England. Car horns honked, vehicles blocked the front of the terminal buildings, parents snatched screaming children from under the wheels of surging taxis. Drivers involved in dramatic family reunions stayed deaf to the shrill of police whistles. The sun was hot. There were no orderly queues. Hamilton threw his bag in the back of a battle-scarred diesel Mercedes and climbed in after it.

"Carlton Hotel."

The driver pulled the meter flag down and nodded. The cab gathered speed with an alarming whine from the rear end. The momentum slammed Hamilton against the patched upholstery. The driver forked right at the end of the approach to the airport, bulling his way out onto a broad thoroughfare lined with apartment buildings. He swayed as he drove, his shoulders reproducing the line he was steering.

"English?"

"No," said Hamilton leaning forward. Marseilles cab-drivers had the reputation of being the worst in the world but Marseilles was never like this. The hack passed traffic on both sides, treating the sidewalk as an extension of the highway. He tried to attract the driver's attention. "Could you take it a little slower, please?"

The man showed gold teeth in the mirror. "Gooda?" he asked, keeping his foot firmly on the gas pedal. It was evident that he had run out of English.

The city grew as they traveled west with every other block gapped by a building site. Giant cranes straddled the excavations like praying mantises. Hamilton's head whipped back as the driver trod hard on his brakes and skidded up to the signals. The red light held them at a vast roundabout with wedding-cake statuary in the center. Railings on the right enclosed the grassy slopes of a park where people sprawled and strolled. The hack jerked his head in the opposite direction.

"Avenida da Liberdade. Carltonotel."

A six-lane highway flanked by mosaic-paved walking spaces dropped down toward the distant gleam of the river. Hamilton had an impression of open-air cafés surrounded by flower beds and trees, of crouching shoeshine boys snapping their rags among outstretched legs. Red changed to green and the rush of vehicles went around anticlockwise as if on rails. Nobody gave quarter, all avoiding collision by a skin of paint. Hamilton's cab pulled out of the suicidal charge at the last moment. The driver skated in front of a bus and stopped suddenly. He was out of his seat, doffing his flat-crowned cap and showing gold teeth as Hamilton opened the door.

"Gooda?" asked the driver, holding up his thumb.

Hamilton's feet found the sidewalk unsteadily. There was something refreshingly innocent in the question. The meter showed that they had covered fourteen kilometers in just under twenty minutes.

"Terrific," he said.

The hotel might have been anywhere in Europe, vast and impersonal, with the usual majestic doorman directing baggage-handlers from the top of black marble steps. To Hamilton's ears the language sounded somewhere between the sounds of a jew's-harp and a buzz saw. Inside the hotel the frenzy of the street was replaced by ordered comfort. Unobtrusive waiters glided through the well-appointed lobby. He carried his blue canvas bag to the reception desk. A black-coated clerk found his name on a list.

"Yes, Mr. Hamilton. Yes, here we are. You're on the second floor at the back. Two-eight-six. You'll find it very quiet. May I have your passport, please?"

Hamilton opened the blue folder at the title page. "I'd like to hang on to this. I have to change traveler's checks at the bank and I need it."

The clerk copied the details onto the printed police form. He closed the passport and returned it with a small bow.

"Thank you, sir. Have a good stay in Lisbon!"

The single room had a large window. The boy pulled up the blinds and put Hamilton's bag on a stand. Hamilton waited at the door till he heard the elevator going down. Rule One in the book was never part with your passport. Rule Two was make sure of an alternative exit. He found the service stairs and followed them down to street level. The exit doors had emergency push-up bars. He could get out but not in. He went up to his room.

The window overlooked the stepped tiled roofs of ancient houses where lines of washing hung above narrow sunless streets. The whole city seemed to be built on hills, the older parts downtown clinging like limpets to slopes that were slashed by broad modern avenues. Flowers grew anywhere they could find foothold. On balconies, windowsills, roof terraces. Every available space had its quota of color. He unpacked his bag and looked for a hiding place for the suede satchel. He finally burrowed under the bed and pulled the carpet away from the wall. The satchel fitted beneath, out of sight. He went into the shower. The cold needles on his back unlocked a memory of an Ontario lake fringed with fir trees, the faintly rotting smell of black water lapping bone-white hoops of beach. He toweled himself with sudden unwonted depression. Every place he had been in his life he seemed to have finally left forever. There was never any going back. Maybe things would be different now. Maybe this money he was getting from Kohn would give him the chance to get things straightened out in his head. At thirty-eight he ought to be able to work out some kind of alternative instead of running like a goddamn fox. He wrapped himself in a dry towel and lay down on the bed feeling sorry for himself.

An hour went by and the phone rang. Kohn sounded as if the flight had affected his breathing.

"I'm glad to hear your voice. Is everything all right?"

"No problems," said Hamilton. "What's on your mind?"

Kohn was wheezing like an elderly bulldog. "Look out of your window. You should be able to see a building with a sign on top that says 'Union Comercial.' Do you see it?"

Hamilton took the phone to the end of the cord. "Got it." The building spiked the ridge of a hill.

"Good," said Kohn. "How soon do you think you could be there?"

Hamilton gauged the distance across the treetops. "I don't know. Twenty minutes, maybe. I'm just out of the shower. I have to dress."

"Well, be as quick as you can. Gunilla works in the building. There's a cafeteria downstairs. Wait for her there. She's going to drive you out so that you can see the place. You understand what I mean?"

Hamilton smiled. Kohn's innuendo thudded in like a well-struck golf ball.

"I understand. I wait in the cafeteria. What sort of car does she drive?"

"A green Volkswagen. We'll all be meeting later this evening. She'll tell you where. Goodbye. Goodbye," he repeated as if fearful of not being heard.

"I'm on my way," said Hamilton. They hadn't even started and Kohn was up-tighter than a snare drum.

He fired the towel into the bathroom and dressed quickly, leaving his overcoat behind. The temperature outside was in the upper fifties. He levered the heavy brass tag from his room key and dropped the tag in a drawer. That was Rule Three, keep your room key on you till you pay your bill. He picked up a street map from the pile on the porter's desk and walked down the steps into dazzling sunlight. The Union Comercial building was clearly marked on his map. He worked his way into a labyrinth of narrow streets where the sun rarely shone, past tall lopsided houses and tiny dark stores smelling of apricots and dried codfish. Cobblers and tinsmiths plied their trades from front-room windows. The occasional open door offered a glimpse of spacious patios belying the external meanness. The crooked lane ended abruptly and he was on a busy avenue. He closed his nose against the sudden stench of diesel fumes. The building he wanted occupied the corner block obliquely across the street. He could see the green signal at the top of the ramp leading down to the subterranean garage. He ducked through the traffic and ran up the steps into the crowded cafeteria. Most of the tables were occupied by teen-age students. He bought himself a beer and a sandwich and carried them to a shelf by the window. The tune bursting out of the jukebox was new to him but it made him feel good. He felt good and he felt confident. The minutes stretched till a green Volkswagen drove up the ramp and stopped at the light. He hurried out. Gunilla von Mayenfels opened the door for him and he slid in beside her.

She was wearing slacks and a scuffed leather jacket. Her bleached-out hair was tied at the back with a blue ribbon and she looked a good five years younger than she had in London. He thought of telling her so and decided against it. Instead he said, "Hi!"

She looked at him soberly with dark blue eyes. "Hello!" She made it sound more of an acknowledgment than a greeting. She gunned the Volkswagen out into the traffic. "I brought a pair of binoculars."

It was a second or two before he understood what she was saying. It was the timing rather than the remark itself. "Hello. I brought a pair of binoculars." Just like that.

He reached back and lifted them from the seat. The dented metal casing bore the insignia of the Luftwaffe. She kicked off her tan buckskins, one after another, managing the controls with strong wrists and bare brown feet. He glanced down curiously.

"Is that the way you always drive?"

"Yes," she said briefly. She handled the car well, meeting bluff and indecision with certainty and judgment. He lit a cigarette and relaxed.

"Know something," he said on impulse. "You ought to try smiling once in a while. You'd be a knockout."

She frowned as if he'd said something that irritated her and turned left at the top of the avenue. A freeway climbed up between groves of pine trees. A sign at the entrance read AUTOSTRADA ESTORIL-SINTRA. She kept the

Volkswagen in the center lane, neither looking at him nor speaking. Beyond the treetops on the left the Salazar suspension bridge spanned the wide silver river. An enormous concrete Christ soared on the opposite bank. Lisbon was something like Vancouver. There was the same nostalgic sight of liners heading for the open sea, the familiar white beauty of the city on the hills behind, the coming and going of ferryboats.

"Pull over," he ordered suddenly.

She swerved into the nearside lane and braked, glancing up at the driving mirror. The cars continued to flick by. Her camel-hair brush eyebrows drew together.

"What was all that about?"

He reached across and turned off the ignition. "I wanted to talk."

She lit a cork-tipped cigarette, watching him over the flame.

"I'm getting bad vibes," he explained. "And I want to know why."

She was wearing a sharp clean scent that somehow went with her patrician manner.

"I'm afraid I don't understand."

"You understand," he said, "and we might as well get a few things straight. You're not entirely sold on the idea of driving me around, right?"

She wriggled her shoulders. "It's strange."

He cocked his head. "Because I'm a thief? But you're just as much a part of this caper as I am. The law calls it conspiracy."

She touched the ribbon at the back of her neck self-consciously. "What exactly is it that you want of me?"

"A smile," he suggested. "I may be a burglar but you'd be surprised what a nice guy I really am."

Her confidence seemed to grow. "Isn't it you who's on the defensive, Mr. Hamilton? Wouldn't it be better to just accept me as I am, the way I've accepted you?"

He shook his head. "But I don't *like* the way you've accepted me! The truth is that you're out of your depth, like Kohn. I'm the only one who isn't. But we're all here for the same thing. Different reasons, maybe, but the same end. That means that we have to have some sort of trust and respect for one another. I don't really care whether or not you approve of me but you've no right to treat me as a monster."

"I suppose not," she said, and then in a low troubled voice, "You know what this means to me. Why wouldn't I trust and respect you? It's just that I've never been much good at showing my feelings."

"Make an effort," he urged. "You could start by calling me Scott. Us burglars aren't usually that formal with our drivers."

Her smile finally broke through. "OK, Scott."

"Much better," he grinned. "In fact, very good. Let it all hang out." He covered her hand with his, a light friendly touch with nothing more behind it and he sensed her response. *"Kamerad?"* he asked.

The skin crinkled at the corners of her eyes. "Of course."

He switched on the motor again and settled back. "OK, driver, let's move it!"

She pointed out the landmarks with a new display of intimacy as if she had made her choice and accepted him.

He was glad of it. She turned the Volks right, leaving the autostrada for the cutoff to Sintra. She swung left again just before Queluz, the small humpbacked car hugging the bends along the narrow lane. Once again it all looked very familiar; the deep canyons and split-level homes camouflaged into the bushy hills could have been located anywhere north of Vancouver. They were somewhere in the mountains between Sintra and Estoril. The speedometer showed that they had covered twenty-two kilometers since leaving Lisbon. The lane dropped abruptly through solid rock that was overgrown with broom and myrtle. A high stone wall came up on their left. She indicated it with her chin.

"That's the beginning of Penha Longa."

The forest of cork oaks opposite reached back as far as the hills they had just come from. A barbed-wire fence protected it from the road. Warnings that no hunting was allowed were posted at regular intervals. Gunilla swung the Volkswagen through a gap where the wire had been flattened and drove in among the trees, rear wheels spinning in the sandy soil. She killed the motor. The last echo died away, leaving the forest silent. There was no movement anywhere and a complete absence of birdsong.

Gunilla used the driving mirror to freshen her lipstick. "We're five hundred meters from the gate lodge. There's only one entrance to the estate."

Their bodies touched as he craned over her shoulder but she made no move to pull away. All he could see was the gray curving wall and the telephone poles along the side of the road.

"You're sure nobody comes in here?" he asked. "Nobody from the estate?"

She shook her head. "I never saw anyone. I used to be here a lot when I worked for Szily."

He glanced across at the still, serried trees. "Alone?"

"Alone." He was right about her smile. The band of freckles shortened across her nose and an unexpected dimple showed up in her chin. He slung the binoculars around his neck.

"Come on, let's explore."

She slipped on her moccasins and followed him to the tree he had chosen. It was a good twenty feet taller than its neighbors. He pointed up through the branches.

"I'll be able to see for miles from the top." He realized that he sounded as if he climbed trees every day and added, "if I ever make it to the top."

The cork had been stripped from the tree exposing a rust-colored slippery surface. He gave her his jacket to hold, tucked his tie in his shirt and gauged the distance to the lowest branch. His first jump was inches short. The second was better and he hung there, legs swinging and tried to chin himself up. The branch sagged and bits of broken bark rained onto his hair and down his neck. His arms trembled with effort as he tried to bring his right leg up over the branch. Suddenly his ankles were grabbed from below and he felt himself lifted. He snatched a fresh hold and was on the branch gazing down into her sweater at firm cupped breasts.

"Thanks!" he gasped. "Now go on back to the car and watch the road."

She moved away, carrying his jacket over her arm. The tree grew straight, its great spread taking its neighbors' light. He went up, straddling the trunk, and wedged himself in the fork at the summit. He had a clear view over the boundary wall. He focused the binoculars until the image stood out sharp and clear. He could see a bridle path beyond the curving wall, the marks of horses' hoofs in the dirt, a glimmer of red roofs through a screen of gum trees. He panned on a shimmer of water and made out a twenty-five-meter pool surrounded by a plate-glass windbreak. Beyond that were palm trees and what looked like a driving range. The red roofs were all he could see of the house itself. The eucalyptus trees made an effective barrier. He made his way down again, dropping the last twenty feet into the yielding soil. He walked over to the Volkswagen brushing the itch from his neck. Gunilla had been watching him from the floor of the car, sitting with her long legs pushed through the open door. His jacket was across her lap. He took it and searched for a smoke.

She smiled as if she was getting the hang of it. "Very impressive. Like Tarzan."

He thumbed a cigarette from the pack and lit it. "How old did you say Szily was?"

"Seventy-three. Why?"

"That's what I thought you said." He blew twin streams of smoke from his nostrils. "So who rides the horses?"

The puzzlement went from her face. "Szily does. He rides for an hour every morning, no matter what sort of weather it is."

He scuffed his shoe through the gray sand. "Know

something? I'd built up this picture of a nice old guy whose idea of sport was a spin in his wheelchair. You've just blown it."

"He's a Balt from Mecklenburg," she said indifferently. "They have salt and wind in their veins and they die standing up."

"Move over," he instructed. She made room for him and they huddled together on the floorboards. "I'm going to need your help."

She helped him get the last of the bark from his neck. "You know I will do it."

It was time for confession, for easing the soul, for making sure that this gallant band of amateurs weren't going to drop him deep in the shit.

"Article number one. I hated that time in jail."

She glanced sideways and nodded. "I can understand. Article number two?"

"I don't want to go back in there. So I'm going to ask you some questions. If you're not absolutely sure about the answers, say so. And I mean sure and then certain. How many of these dogs are there over there?"

"Two. Doberman pinschers."

"And where would they be right now? No guesses, remember."

She answered again with assurance. "In the kennels. They're kept there till dark, then the gardener turns them loose."

Eyes glared from a snarling mask. He felt the agonizing cramps as some clown gave him anti-rabies shots.

"You mean people go there for dinner and run the risk of going home minus a limb?"

"No." She shook her head. "There are no guests at night, or rarely, and very few during the day. The mail and supplies are left at the lodge and the gates are locked at six every night."

The thought opened a door in his mind and he saw an Ascot garden party with striped marquees on the lawn, champagne bottles popping, the chatter of well-bred voices drifting up through the open window as he prowled through the master bedroom. He had come and gone unnoticed, mingling with the guests, the contents of the hostess's jewelbox in his pockets. The miniature-wheeled bicycle he had used to approach the house carried him the two miles to his parked car, where he stowed it neatly in the trunk.

"Have you got a pen and paper?" he asked suddenly.

She reached for her purse in the glove compartment and offered a diary with a pencil attached. He flipped over to a blank page.

"Draw me a plan of the house."

She sketched competently, blocking in a rambling structure surrounding an inner courtyard. She tore off the page and drew the same thing in elevation. Then she added a scale and marked two points with an X.

"This is the museum and that is Szily's bedroom."

She was close and her scent reminded him of it. He pursed his lips, studying the sketches carefully.

"You're sure this is accurate?"

"Absolutely. That building on the right is the guesthouse. The secretary's flat is above the garage." Her brown capable forefinger stabbed at the piece of paper. "And the servants sleep here—the kitchen staff, the gardeners, the groom and the chauffeur. There are fourteen people working on the estate including the gatekeeper and his wife."

He traced a triangle. "How do they communicate with one another?"

Her shoulders were on the bony side but she had an elegant shrug.

"There is a house phone with an automatic switchboard. It connects all the rooms in the big house with the rest of the place."

He stuffed the pieces of paper in his pocket. "You and I should have gotten together sooner."

She made no reply and he looked to see why. The closed-in look was back on her face.

"I wish you'd stop acting as though you're leading some sort of freak through the jungle. I want you to clear my father's name. I don't care about the pats on the back."

The suddenness of the outburst surprised him. "What's the matter with you again? Are you crazy or something?"

Her dark blue eyes held steady then finally surrendered. "I'm nervous and I'm scared and I'm sorry. Is that enough apology?"

"Handsome," he said, and threw the binoculars on the back seat. "I'm not quite certain what Kohn expected from this expedition, some kind of instant revelation from the top of a tree maybe, or didn't he say?"

A faint flush still backed her freckles. "I think he assumed that you would know what to do."

There was a challenge in her eyes. He felt that it was time to step on stage and do his number.

"I'm going over that wall," he said steadily. "I'll need

your help. If I'm not back in an hour's time, get hold of Kohn and tell him what happened." The statement had a good dramatic ring to it and he hoped he was only kidding. Four hours in someone else's country and here he was proposing to skulk through the woods like a poacher.

He took hold of her arm and pulled her up. Something whirred in the bush as they neared the road. He ducked instinctively and froze. She shook her head, smiling. Seconds later a hoopoe's call sounded and a golden bird flashed down the road to perch on the telephone pole, its crest erect. Insects droned in the February sunshine, the wild flowers were sweetly scented. The road as far as the eye could see was deserted.

"Do you think you can hold my weight?" he demanded.

"I just did it," she reminded and bent low, bracing her legs.

He climbed up onto her back and knelt with his palms flat against the wall. He could feel her body shaking.

"Straighten up," he instructed.

Her legs wobbled but she made it. He brought up one foot after another with infinite care till he was standing on her shoulders. His fingers grasped the stonework then a quick heave had him lying along the top of the wall. He showed her his thumb and dropped down on the other side. He crouched, waiting, till he heard her run across the road. Then he moved backward across the bridle path, obliterating his footmarks in the dirt as he went. The smell of eucalyptus was strong. The gray twisted leaves shivered under his passage and the silence was uncanny. He dragged a stout fallen branch from the undergrowth and marked the spot in his mind. It was strong enough to help him back over the wall. The red roofs were much closer now. He could count six of them, sloping at different angles, with the eaves turned up like Chinese pagodas. Suddenly he could see the house, surrounded by banana palms. The gum trees stopped at the edge of the graveled driveway. He pulled Gunilla's sketches from his pocket and went down on his stomach. The driveway curled off left to the front of the house. Szily's bedroom was somewhere there on the second story. A glass dome bulged above the tiles, behind the hidden patio. According to Gunilla, the dome provided the museum with its only source of natural light. All the windows appeared to be covered with wrought-iron grilles. He lifted himself on his elbows and followed the line of the wall in front to an open door.

He tore the sketches up and thumbed them deep into the soft earth. A sharp crack echoed through the spinney, the sound coming from the direction of the driving range. Dogs started to yelp somewhere off to the left. He clambered up, brushing the dirt from his knees and elbows and backed off, keeping in the shelter of the trees. A man dressed in an old-fashioned knickerbocker suit came into sight striding across the grass, carrying a golf stick over his shoulder. He was obviously making for a white flag that was three hundred yards or so away. Hamilton whipped around as footsteps crunched across the gravel behind him. An overweight man with flat shiny hair came down the driveway, wearing a striped toweling robe and whistling. He trotted across the thatch of Bermuda grass and down the steps leading to the sunken pool. A splash followed. He reappeared quickly to lie flat on his back with his face to the waning sun.

Hamilton glanced across at the open side door. He'd never get another chance like this. The two men he had just seen were obviously Szily and the secretary. All he had to do now was locate the servants. He checked his watch, staring at the dial with disbelief. Ten after five. Only twelve minutes had passed since he had dropped over the wall. He ran along the grass verge to the front of the house. He was out of sight of the driving range and the pool. Granite steps ascended to a massive porch flanked by stone bears. The sound of women's voices came plainly in the still air from the direction of the servants' quarters. Someone was running a power mower on the far side of the terraced rose garden.

He wiped the back of his hand across his mouth, trying to reach a decision. Going through that door was only the beginning. The museum was clear across the house and that was what he needed to see. He moved back warily and peeked through a barred window. The last of the sun lingered in the interior patio. Bougainvillea colored the field-stone walls. A green-and-yellow parrot was dozing on its perch in the middle of the courtyard. The sound of another ball being driven gave him fresh confidence and he tiptoed along the wall to the side entrance. There were two doors, not one; the space between them a place for coats and walking sticks. The outer door had bolts and two mortise locks; the inner was a swing door sealed with felt. He pushed both open gently and stepped into an enormous room that ran from one side of the house to the other.

Two fringed velvet couches faced an open fireplace where logs lay ready to be lighted. Carved deep into the mantel were the words

NON OMNIA MORAR

Blue chairs matched the couches and the walls were hung with somber Dutch landscapes where stolid-looking men and women skated red-faced among frozen poplars. Potpourri strewn in Sevres bowls made the room fragrant. Hamilton stepped across the antique Tabriz carpet and went as far as the window. It overlooked the pool and the driving range. He could see Szily swinging his golf stick in the distance. The secretary was still flat on his back at the edge of the water, eyes shut.

The grilles on the window were as much for protection as decoration and were sunk deep in the masonry. Cutting through the ironwork would be both noisy and arduous. He walked back to the outer of the two doors he had come through. He wrapped his handkerchief around the key and eased it out of the lock. The basic pattern of the wards was a dropped-E. He slipped the key back in the lock and measured the position of the bolts. One was six inches from the top of the door, the other the same distance from the ground. Everything would depend on whether or not the key was left in the lock at night. Gunilla's information had been on the button so far. He backed off, opened the door at the end of a corridor and tiptoed down it between gilt-and-plaster saints standing on pedestals. The library was opposite the patio and furnished with dark heavy pieces. English, German and Portuguese newspapers were piled on a refectory table. Nearby was a carved-wood lectern in the form of an eagle with outstretched wings supporting a copy of the *Almanach de Gotha.* He stepped between the lectern and table, ducking behind the tapestry as a door opened along the corridor. He pressed himself flat against steel as he heard the footsteps and the woman's voice. The heavy tapestry smelled musty and he wanted to sneeze. The library windows were barred like the rest. There was no escape. He was totally committed. The Portuguese jabber grew fainter and he suddenly understood. The woman was in the patio talking to the parrot. He heard the scrape of metal on stone as she moved the bird's stand. The footsteps retreated and the house was quiet again. The pungent smell of woodsmoke invaded the library. The fire had been lighted, a sign, perhaps, that Szily was expected back. The sooner he got out of there, the better. He pushed the tapestry aside and took a good look at the door to the museum. It hung on overhead rollers, the power-driven mechanism controlled by a small cylindrical lock. A plate beneath read

ROSSITER SECURITY SYSTEMS L2

He stepped away, letting the tapestry fall back in place. There wasn't a man alive who could pick a lock like that. Short of a thermal lance the manganese steel was impregnable. The only thing going for him was the fact that the L2 models weren't fitted with time devices. The corridor was quiet. He crept back to the drawing room like a cat crossing a wet street. Olive branches were crackling in the fireplace and the parrot was on its stand by a window. It shuffled to the end of its perch, head cocked forbiddingly as Hamilton made his way toward the side door. The coast outside was clear and he ran as hard as he could go for the shelter of the eucalyptus trees. He found his branch and used it to clamber up the wall. He threw the branch back into the trees and dropped smoothly down onto the road. Gunilla had brought the Volkswagen closer and opened the door to let him in. He leaned on the side of the car trying to get his breath. He looked up from his scuffed shoes and stuck a cigarette between his lips. It was his first smoke in an hour and he needed it. She offered a match. He dragged deep and exhaled.

"I was inside the house."

The sun had dipped low and dappled light fell across her face. *"Inside?"*

There was a note of amazement that pleased him. They wanted derring-do, then, sir, he'd give it to them.

"That's right. How often does Szily go into the museum?"

She started cleaning the dirt from his jacket with her handkerchief.

"I've never been there at night, but according to the servants he goes in there every evening after dinner. He takes a glass of brandy with him and sometimes sits there for hours. They can see the light in the dome long after they've gone to bed."

He had a clear picture of Szily in evening clothes, erect in his chair, gloating over his possessions.

"Does he sleep alone?"

She looked at him, astounded. "How do you mean? He's a bachelor."

"Come off it," he said impatiently. "It's been known for a bachelor to sleep with his servants."

"Not Baron Szily."

"OK. But since we're on the subject I'd like to ask you a personal question."

Whatever else, she was no coward. "If it'll help you to help me."

"It just might," he answered. "I want to know if there's a man in your life. Someone who might turn out to be more important to you than I am. I'm talking about my safety."

She spoke in a small tight voice. "There is only one man in my life. Your safety means the chance to clear his name. Does that answer your question?"

He pitched the half-smoked butt through the open window. The trees gave off a vinegary smell. A car droned by on the road. He watched its progress as far as the bend.

"I think I can beat that place," he said quietly. "It won't be easy but what we have here is a man who thinks he's infallible. That helps. Every time he rolls that door shut at night something turns off in his brain. The buck is passed to a slab of steel and the dogs. That's where he's wrong."

Her expression was doubtful. "You're not thinking of cutting the power supply? There's an auxiliary generator."

"No, I am not thinking of the power supply. If you cut it the door won't move an inch. You say Szily keeps the key to the museum in his bedroom?"

"The servants said so. I heard him say as much once to the secretary. It was something to do with fire."

"It's logical," he said. "So I'll take it from his bedroom."

Her fingers flew to her throat. "But *how?* He could wake up!"

"Trust the man at the wheel," he said. "I've seen all I need to see. Waiting makes me nervous. I'm going to tell Kohn that we go tomorrow night and I'd like you to drive me. Would you do that, Gunilla?"

"I'll do it."

"You won't be scared?"

"I'll be scared but I'll do it. We're supposed to meet Kohn at eight-thirty. The Bar Fronteira. It's only about ten minutes' walk from your hotel. The other man's going to be there, the one from Paris."

He looked at his watch. "Could you drive me somewhere now? How about your job?"

"I'm off sick," she told him. "Where do you want to be driven?"

"Some place I can buy a rabbit. A wild rabbit."

She looked at him open-mouthed, then started to giggle. After a while she straightened up and wiped her eyes. The handkerchief she used was the one she had cleaned his jacket with. It left streaks of dirt across her face.

"I'm sorry," she gasped. "It was the way you said it. You looked so serious."

"I *am* serious," he insisted.

She found a tissue and dabbed her eyes again, using the driving mirror.

"My maid would probably know. We'll catch her at the house if we hurry. Does it have to be wild?"

"Wild, scared and a long-distance runner."

She stuffed the tissue into the ashtray.

"You've asked me a lot of questions. I'd like to ask you one."

He waved a hand. "Help yourself."

Her voice was suddenly awkward. "How does a man like you become a thief?"

He combed his hair with his fingers, wondering what he should answer. People had been asking him the same question for the past three years.

"Well, I'll tell you. I think I'm going to pass on that one. It's not as simple as it sounds."

Her eyes were frank and steady. "You could try. I never met anyone like you before."

"What did you expect?" he asked, smiling. "Some kind of a monster? I was brought up in a Catholic reform school."

A nerve jumped in her fine-skinned throat. "You're as much on the defensive as I am, aren't you? I think you're a good man."

"So are you," he said. "Let's go find that rabbit."

She kicked off her shoes and drove the car out through the gap in the wire. She turned it west at Queluz onto a replica of the road they had just left. It descended toward the ocean through deep cuts in the rocky hillside. She answered his questions readily, as if his right to ask them had been established beyond doubt. The house they were going to now had been her aunt's; it was a converted fisherman's cottage, the only home she had ever known. A child's longing and an old maid's loyalty had fashioned a dream that was to last through the years. Her father was alive somewhere in South America and as soon as his name had been cleared he'd return. Cards and presents arrived from Brazil, the messages signed in his name. She was nineteen when her aunt died. Gunilla had gone through the old woman's papers, finding a box of letters written in the same hand as her father's. Only this time the signature was different, Hugo Bayer. She read the letters and understood. Bayer was Evangelical pastor to the German community in Santos and a childhood friend of her aunt's. It was Bayer who had sent the gifts and the letters.

Hamilton's wish to comfort was instinctive. "That's one hell of a story. Do you still think your father's alive?"

Her voice was tight and controlled. "My mother died in childbirth, giving him the daughter he always said he wanted. Now I'm almost thirty years old and I don't remember the sound of his voice. He has to be dead. It's his reputation I care about."

Whitewashed houses and a pink church hugged the hillside below. Fishing boats were beached in the hoop of harbor. The road dropped straight into a square shaded by mulberry trees where dogs dozed among the fruit and vegetable stands. A fountain jetted listlessly out of a tangled mess of nasturtiums. They climbed up past the church into a cobbled alley, flat-eared cats crouching over fish carcasses. The walls closed in, reeking of ammonia, till there was barely room for the car to scrape through and then suddenly they were shooting down a narrow street that followed the line of the headland. She cut the motor and nodded over at a blue door flanked by tubs filled with geraniums.

"That's me."

The ocean boomed in the caves below. Dirt and refuse caked the fronts of deserted summer houses. Gunilla touched the horn-ring. A woman in a black dress opened the door. Gunilla spoke in Portuguese and the maid came out and planted solid legs, looking at Hamilton with open curiosity. Gunilla opened her door.

"She says that she knows someone. A woman who lives around the corner. Her son sets snares."

Faces peered from behind curtains as they went down the street. The maid kept looking sideways at Hamilton and giggling. She led the way into a yard behind a ramshackle building and announced her arrival with a shrill scream. An old woman shuffled out, humpbacked and wrapped in a rusty black shawl. The yard stank of manure and rotting vegetation. Hens were scratching through dank cabbage leaves. The crone lifted a shaking arthritic hand, pointing at the homemade hutch against the crumbling wall.

"She says her son caught it early this morning."

Hamilton bent down and peeked through the chicken wire. A brown-gray buck crouched on powerful hindquarters, looking up at him with twitching nose.

"That's a hare, not a rabbit," he said.

Her face fell. "You mean it's no good?"

"Give grandma the money. We'll go back to your place." He found a carton, punched some holes in its side, tipped the hare into it and tied the box with a string.

The three women watched with interest. The buck was kicking hard inside.

Gunilla spoke to the maid who scurried away. The curtains twitched again as she walked Hamilton up to the blue door. The room inside had a low ceiling, french windows and rough whitewashed walls. Steps beyond the french windows led down to a tiny garden under the spread branches of an old vine. A door at the end of the garden offered direct access to the cliff and a path to the cove below. The oak table and heavy tallboy were plainly German. There were three basket armchairs, a battered silver vase filled with bronze chrysanthemums and faded rugs on the scrubbed brick floor. The fireplace was laid with driftwood bleached by the salt and sun.

"That's all there is," she said. "Two small bedrooms, a bathroom, a kitchen and this."

"I like it," he said, looking around. The place had a comfortable lived-in feeling.

She untied the ribbon and shook her hair free. "Do you mind telling me what you intend doing with that animal you're holding?"

He undid the french windows and went down some steps to a kind of shed with gardening implements inside. He left the carton on the floor and turned the key in the lock. All he could see from where he stood was a waste of white-flecked water extending as far as the horizon. Far out, an ocean-going liner seemed pasted motionless against the sky. She was a strange girl, living what was practically a nun's life, defending frontiers that nobody attacked, staring out to sea while ghosts rapped on the windows. He walked back into the house. Flames were licking up the smoke-blackened chimney. Gunilla had brushed her hair and used her lipstick. He sank down in one of the basket chairs.

"That animal, as you call it, is going to save our lives with any sort of luck."

"You mean the dogs?" Frown marks gathered on her forehead. "They'll just tear it to pieces."

He moved his finger from side to side. "It takes two to tango."

"But the noise," she objected. "You'll wake the whole household."

The climb had left his arms aching and he slumped down, pushing his legs out.

"Have you finished?"

She made a face at him. "I've finished."

He looked at her over his clasped hands. "Then listen to me on the subject of wildlife. A hare can run the legs off any dog except a greyhound and even then it has a fifty-fifty chance. Those woods around Penha Longa are full of rabbit droppings. The dogs must have gotten the scent and gone off hunting a hundred times. As for the noise, Dobermans aren't foxhounds. They don't waste their breath on the run. There'll be no noise that Szily and the servants haven't heard before."

She lit a cigarette from the fire. "Is that just guesswork or do you really know about these things?"

"Let's say it's a combination of both. I'm a country boy. There's room for the hare to maneuver and run, two hundred hectares. And I'm going to make sure that the dogs get the scent." He tapped the side of his nose.

She glanced away through the french windows. "You mean you want me to keep that thing *here?*"

"I've locked the door. It's not going anywhere even if it eats its way out of the carton."

She pantomimed a shiver. "I don't want to touch it. Would you like something to drink? There's not much, I'm afraid. I can offer you tea, coffee or *madronho*."

The word was unfamiliar. "What the hell is *madronho?*"

She took a bottle out of the tallboy. It bore no label and the liquid inside was colorless. He pulled the cork and sniffed cautiously. It smelled like fusel oil.

"They distill it from the fruit of the arbutus tree," she volunteered.

He touched the cork with the tip of his tongue and wiped his hand across his mouth.

"I'll settle for coffee."

She returned the bottle to its place. "I won't be a minute."

He heard her in the kitchen and reflected that it would have been good to stay here for a while with the fire burning in the gathering darkness and talk. He had a hunch that Gunilla would make a good listener and there was one thing that they had in common, loneliness. She came back, carrying an earthenware pot and cups and a plate of cookies. She pushed a table between their chairs, put the tray on it and poured coffee.

"The cookies are coconut. I made them myself."

The monogrammed napkin she had given him was darned but spotless. He sipped the strong sweet Angolan coffee and closed his mouth on a cookie.

"Very good indeed!"

"I'm glad you like them." Her diffidence failed to hide her pleasure. She sat down, balancing her cup on her knee. "Shall I tell you something, you frightened me to death in London. All I knew about you was what Kohn had said and even your smile was somehow sinister. Now I think I understand you. In a way I wish that I didn't. It's given me something else to worry about. It's hard for me to explain but I feel responsible."

He set his plate down carefully. "Don't. In a few hours I'll be on my way."

Her eyes were free of coquetry. "You're a strange man, do you know that? I'm going to find it hard to forget you."

"You'll forget," he assured her. "In the meantime don't start feeling sorry or responsible for me. I'm the way that I am and its nobody's business but mine. OK?"

"It isn't just the money, is it?" she demanded.

He moved a shoulder. "What else?" In a sense it was false for whatever was left of her dream he wanted preserved. He changed the subject deliberately. "What does that motto mean over Szily's fireplace?"

She thought for a minute. "Something like 'I shall not die completely.' It's not a perfect translation but it's near enough."

He thumbed a cigarette up from the pack. "Nobody dies completely."

A log collapsed, showering the chimney with sparks. "Have you always been so sure of yourself?" she asked quietly. "I mean in the past."

"I guess most of it's wishful thinking. A dream you want to come true."

She nodded as if she understood. "I'd like to show you a picture of my father." She opened a drawer in the tall-boy.

The photograph she handed to Hamilton showed a blond man in diplomatic uniform. His eyes offered the same blue challenge as hers. He gave her back the picture.

"A handsome man."

She changed the subject as easily as he did. "How you must have hated prison."

He turned the corners of his mouth down. "I admit it gave me quite a turn."

"What was worst?"

He put his mind in reverse. "It was all bad. Tomorrow was the same as yesterday. There was squalor and a total loss of dignity. Enough?"

She leaned back, long-legged and desirable in a tom-boyish way. "How about a loss of love?"

There was something almost aggressive in her tone and he sat up straighter.

"You're asking some pretty heavy questions, aren't you?"

"Why not?" she answered. "You asked me enough. The men in my life and the rest. Come on, tell me about love in prison. Do the little women wait or does love just die of slow strangulation?"

He glanced up at her, half-smiling. "Sometimes it gets the chop right at the beginning. Then it's easier all around."

She nibbled at a piece of skin on her finger, keeping her eyes fixed on his face.

"In spite of that pose, in spite of what you say, you're a romantic. That's how she was able to hurt you so badly, whoever she was."

The stale memory left him unmoved. "On the contrary, the lady had a heart of gold. I think it's about time you took me back to my hotel."

IV

THE HEADQUARTERS of the Direccão-Geral de Segurança were in a gloomy stucco building near the San Carlos Theater. Forbidding doors, seemingly permanently shut, gapped the walls and radio masts poked from the roof. Most of the windows were both filthy and barred. Plainclothesmen dressed like professional mourners lounged in the entrance hall, scanning the nervous civilians from behind dark glasses.

Ilifio Fonseca Machado bounced in with the springy gait of a mountaineer. He was a stockily built man in his fifties, dressed in the uniform black suit and tie. Protruding teeth and eyeballs gave him a look of permanent surprise. His iron-gray hair had been trimmed to an inch-long bristle. He hurried through waiting rooms that were sour with the stench of fear and frustration, past an armed guard and along a maze of passages to a flight of stone steps. His office was an oblong room on the second story. The sign on the door said

INSPECTOR-SUPERVISOR MACHADO

The windows overlooked the fountain in the square in front of the theater. Machado had scratched a peephole in the paint that covered the lower panes. In moments of stress he liked to watch the urchins playing beneath the jacaranda tree. The office was sparsely furnished, no more than a desk with three telephones, a row of metal filing cabinets and a horsehair sofa he had found in one of the storerooms. On the desk by the phones was a colored photograph of an enormously fat woman with beautiful features. Machado unlocked a filing cabinet, tossed a folder onto the desk and touched a button.

A bald man with acne-scarred cheeks appeared in the doorway of the neighboring room and stood at strict attention.

"Senhor Cabo!"

"Chief" was a term used with affection throughout Machado's command.

Machado scratched a match across the base of the lamp in front of him. He applied the flame to the end of his cheroot, looking at his aide. Pacheco's jacket carried traces of the meal he had cooked on the premises and his clothes looked as if he'd bought them in some riverside slop-shop. Machado had come across him working in Records, checked him out and found that Pacheco had a reputation of being a religious-minded bachelor whose sole idea of loose living was to go roller-skating. After a trial period Machado had promoted him, making him his personal assistant. In return for the confidence expressed in him, Pacheco offered a spaniel's devotion and the memory of a computer.

Machado pointed a square-nailed finger. "Have you looked at yourself in the mirror recently?"

Pacheco glanced down, his pitted cheeks coloring, and brushed the dried egg from his lapel.

"An oversight, Senhor Cabo. I am sorry. Inspector Cabral asked to be informed as soon as you arrived. He is upstairs in the armory."

Machado pushed the green phone across the desk. "Then inform him."

Pacheco spoke briefly before cradling the receiver. "He is on his way down. I have the report on Kosky, Senhor. He is at the Hotel Mondial, room forty-two."

Machado scribbled the number on a pad. "Book a room on the same floor. Use the name Martins. Do the people at the airport know that this business is top-security?"

Pacheco's eyes were as round and unblinking as an owl's. *"Si,* Senhor. I told Inspector Duarte that your interest is personal. No one else at headquarters knows of Kosky's arrival."

Machado spit a shred of tobacco into the ashtray. The filling of his cheroot was loose. Nobody wanted to do a good job any longer, even the cigar-makers in the Açores.

"That's all," he said. "I'll have a word with you after

I've spoken to Inspector Cabral. And don't forget the room at the Mondial."

He stared at the closing door through a haze of tobacco smoke. He had commanded the department since its inception, reluctantly at first and finally more or less on his own terms. Centrintel was a concept of centralized intelligence conceived by the Minister of Justice himself. Until then, the subversive activities of Portuguese and foreign nationals had been handled by three different agencies, each working for its own ends. Centrintel had been given authority to handle all such cases that were not the specific concern of the armed forces. Machado's approach had been radical, his requirements unequivocal. He demanded direct access to the Council of Ministers when necessary, freedom from bureaucratic interference and the right to choose his own men.

He stuck his finger into his right ear and oscillated it vigorously. A single failure could easily blot out a string of successes but his feeling was strong about Kosky. He pushed his chair back, as a tall man with a long narrow head and a jutting nose poked his head around the door. Cabral was wearing a gray overcheck suit cut in English fashion and elegant shoes strapped to a high polish. He lifted a gloved right hand in salute, showing good strong teeth.

"Senhor Cabo!"

Machado indicated the horsehair sofa. "Sit down, Luis!" Sometimes he thought of Cabral as the son who had been denied him. Cabral's record since he had joined Centrintel was a formidable one. Born on a Moçambique tea plantation, he'd been orphaned at the age of eleven, his father, mother and grandparents chopped to pieces by terrorist pangas. Ten minutes' butchery had wiped out three generations of courage and endeavor. Cabral had been left for dead, the nerves and sinews of his right hand destroyed. A hatred of Communists, and a ferocity of purpose had made a policeman out of him, maimed as he was. He'd been Machado's man for the last three years.

Machado tapped the file in front of him. "We have a guest. Senhor Marco Orlando Kosky arrived in Lisbon this afternoon from Paris."

Cabral looked up quickly from his fingernails. "*Kosky?* I find that hard to believe."

Machado waved his dead cheroot. "Nevertheless, it's true. There's no question of it. He's traveling under his own name and the passport number checks. He's at the Mondial Hotel."

Cabral's dark stare was disconcerting. "And what are we doing about it?"

"Investigating, Luis." Machado scraped his chair back. "I've just left the secretariat. Senhor Bello was his usual evasive self. We have a completely free hand, always remembering the government's concern with the rights of foreigners."

Cabral's mouth grew thin. "I didn't know that scum like Kosky *had* any rights in Portugal."

Machado wagged his head behind upraised finger. "He's carrying a valid French passport. The thing to discover is *why* he is here."

Cabral shrugged. "I give you one guess. He's an explosives expert."

"Was," corrected Machado.

He opened the file on the desk and studied the picture inside. The fellow had the eyes of a brothel keeper. News came and went quickly since the Luso-Brazilian police accord. The affair of the kidnaped Swiss had been fully documented. The ambassador had been seized outside his house, bundled into a truck like an animal and held for seventy days in a succession of hideouts. His abductors demanded the release of nine violent and dangerous rebels imprisoned by the Brazilian authorities. Kosky had been one of them. The government's surrender to blackmail left Machado with a feeling of personal indignation.

He planted both elbows on the desk. "Let me refresh your memory about this charmer.

KOSKY, MARCO ORLANDO born Santos 5/6/34. Occupation photographical laboratory assistant. Married, wife's whereabouts unknown. One meter sixty-two centimeters, brown hair and eyes, no distinguishing marks or peculiarities. Approximate weight sixty-two kilograms. KOSKY joined A.R.A. Armed Revolutionary Action) March 1956. He is known to have supplied chemicals used in the manufacture of explosive devices. KOSKY is believed to have developed the so-called "butterfly bomb" responsible for the deaths of Police Colonel Nelson Garcia and family. KOSKY was arrested 8/1/69 and held in the Ave Maria barracks in Rio de Janeiro, released 3/19/70 by Presidential decree together with eight other criminal subversives. KOSKY left Brazil 3/20/70, arriving in France via Mexico 3/24/70. Subject founded QUESTOR S.A., a private inquiry agency with premises at 285 bis Rue Sébastopol, Paris, where he resides. Analysis of data available to this office suggests that KOSKY may be reclassified as "nonactive." He acquired French nationality

10/2/73 and was issued with a French passport on that date. (No. 64572345).

The stationery was that of the Brazilian Federal Police.

Machado's face was sly. "Who would have thought he'd turn up in Lisbon?"

Cabral picked a shred of lint from his sock. "I suppose we could say that you did. Those descriptions have been at the frontier posts for more than a year."

Machado dropped his soggy cheroot in a cuspidor filled with an evil-looking liquid.

"Do you know *why,* Luis? Because I don't believe that there is any such animal as a dedicated Communist on the nonactive list. I'll take that further, especially someone like Kosky."

Cabral reversed the file, opened it again and studied the photograph inside.

"May I make an observation?"

"I'd be disappointed if you didn't," Machado said drily.

Cabral spoke with telling assurance. "There *is* no real Communist party in Portugal. There are the radical-chic, as the Americans call them, and a few dissident students in Lisbon and Coimbra. Students have always demonstrated against something or other. I did myself."

Machado was decorating the edges of his blotter with an old-fashioned fountain pen. He was proud of Cabral's education and in a perverse sort of way proud of his own lack of it, which made his own achievements seem to him to be the greater.

"I believe you threw a few stink bombs. It is hardly the same thing."

Cabral's long head bounced the answer away. "We Portuguese have a history of rebellions without causes. We're *all* potential dictators. We need strong handling to avoid a state of anarchy. Salazar understood it. He knew that for us democracy was a dangerous and outdated dogma."

Machado beat his palms together softly. "Bravo, Luis! Continue."

Cabral recrossed his legs, showing a length of gray cashmere sock. "The Communist party here is a dragon without a head. Kosky's no fool. He knows it. He has come here openly and I don't believe it's to blow up bridges."

Machado screwed the cap on his fountain pen. "Then why *has* he come?"

Cabral lit a cigarette one-handed. "Kosky the adventurer. Kosky the private detective. But not as Kosky the Communist."

Machado beamed approval. "I agree. That is why you and I are going to determine the nature of this private business. You have a room on the same floor as his at the Hotel Mondial. You are Senhor Martins. I want to know what Kosky does. And I want him to feel secure. Use as few men as possible and be discreet."

Cabral came to his feet, his hooked nose dominating his profile. "I like it. It'll get me out of this depressing building." He stared at the painted windows, the cuspidor, and shuddered.

Machado came around the desk and touched Cabral on the shoulder. "Such elegance! You don't even *look* like a policeman. I'll use the name Santos if I call you at the hotel. I have a feeling about this one, Luis. A feeling in my bones."

"It's probably rheumatism," Cabral said, poker-faced. He smiled suddenly and the effect was disconcerting. "I'll be in touch."

Machado shut the door behind him and locked Kosky's file away. Pacheco answered the buzzer.

"I have to go out," said Machado.

"Si, Senhor Cabo." The lapels of Pacheco's jacket had been thoroughly cleaned. "I am making a list of all foreigners who have checked into the hotels and *pensions* today. I will study this list and make an analysis." He tapped the side of his nose expressively.

"Do that," said Machado. Pacheco's devotion to duty made him a prey to anxiety and he was constantly on the alert to prove himself. He tried to click his heels and failed. "We are too old for gymnastics," Machado said benevolently. "Let the brain do the work."

The small black Renault outside was without police markings. He drove it uptown as quickly as he could, as always disgusted by what he saw. A country whose sailors had mapped the world had been reduced to playing innkeeper to the riffraff of Europe. Village dancers made idiots of themselves in the sacred name of folklore. *Fadistas* sang of a Lisbon that no longer existed. A country that catered to foreigners was a country without a backbone. The truth was that the real spirit of Portugal lived on in the mountains. Wherever the fight was waged against terrorism, in Moçambique, Angola or Guiné, it was the mountaineers who made the best soldiers. The townsfolk had been completely corrupted.

He turned the car onto the Sintra highway, his mind leaping ahead of him. Just a few more years and he would retire, close his office for the last time and receive the customary accolade from the Minister in person. Then Luisa and he would head south for São João da Serra, the village where he had been born. Even the name was invigorating. A pleateau covered with thyme, rosemary and heather, high in the mountains, a hundred years away from the follies of Lisbon. His mother had been the village schoolmistress and the stone-built house was still his, redolent with the smell of the carob beans that his cousin stored there. A spring gushed from the rocks behind the house and became a stream that meandered by the side of the one paved road. Everything up there was pure: the air, the water and even the souls of men — or so his mother had claimed. Imagination bounded to the time when he would join the old men playing dominoes in the *tasca,* surrounded by the smell of strong wine and goat cheese. He would fish for trout in the deep, dark-brown pools and hunt rabbits instead of human beings. He found the prospect pleasing.

The village where Machado now lived was too far from the coast to be fashionable. It was the kind of place where men in pajamas hung over garden gates on Sunday mornings watching their families on the way to mass in a pink stucco church that smelled mysteriously of monkeys. In the nine years that the Machados had lived in Sacotes they had never put foot in any house other than their own. Machado passed locally for an inspector of television licenses. The cover allowed both for his air of authority and the hours he kept.

He turned the car right at the plastic café opposite the railroad station and aimed it down a lane bordered by budding almond trees. In the south they would soon be in bloom. An undistinguished cement bungalow stood on a slope where the lane stopped. A large black limousine was drawn up on the grass verge outside. The chauffeur was wearing oversize sunglasses and reading comics. The garden gate was wide open. Machado closed it behind him and walked to the back of the bungalow. Chrysanthemums grew in the lee of the high wall. He had always done well with his flowers though fruit seemed to defeat him. Worms got into the pears and children raided the strawberry beds. Luisa was too fat to catch them and too indulgent to complain to their parents. It was almost six o'clock. The last of the sun reddened the top of the west wall. A man emerged from the shade of the pear tree. Like Machado, dressed completely in black, he was smiling under a wide-brimmed hat. He shook hands like a priest, his grip soft and without either beginning or end. "I apologize, Excellency." A certain combination of sibilants made Machado spray. He averted his head, aware of it. "The traffic was heavy."

His visitor seemed to hear from a far distance. "It is of small importance. May we go inside?"

Machado hurried to lead the way. His telephoned instructions had stipulated an empty house. He had sent Luisa to the movies. He had met the man behind him on three previous occasions, each time in the private offices of the Minister of Justice. Senhor Lobo was an anonymous observer with an undefined purpose whose decisions were nonetheless made with authority. He was also one of the five so-called Inspectors of Cause, a shadowy agency instituted by Salazar and responsible solely to the President of the Republic. Machado opened his front door and bowed his guest in. There was a bowl of wild hyacinths on top of the refrigerator. Luisa always said that the kitchen was the place for the refrigerator but it had been thus in his mother's time and he saw no reason for change. He waited till Lobo was safely seated then sat in his own chair. Lobo was an *"alta personalidade"* and you didn't offer people of his quality a glass of wine. Scotch whisky probably, but then Machado had none. He inclined his head.

"Excellency?"

Lobo covered his knees with his wide-brimmed hat. "You understand, Inspector, that there were reasons for asking you to receive me like this?"

Machado licked his front teeth. It was like asking if he understood the necessity for breathing.

"Naturally, Senhor."

Lobo's smile came and went. "I am here on a matter of extreme delicacy. A matter that you have been chosen to deal with in person. Congratulations."

"I shall do my best to merit Your Excellency's confidence in me." And, *mierda,* he added in his mind.

Lobo's gaze was contemplative. "Naturally I consulted your Minister. He agreed with my suggestion that the assignment should supersede any other work that you might have in hand. Do you still have Cabral in your command?"

"Yes, Excellency."

"Well there you are," Lobo said expressively. "Anything important can be left in his hands. It's often good to delegate authority."

The urbane phrases fell on Machado's ears like lead weights. Of course the Minister had been consulted and of course he had agreed. What else? Kosky's face floated away grinning. Lobo reached inside his jacket and extracted a long brown envelope. He placed it on top of his hat.

"Do you know who Baron Szily is, Inspector?"

Machado inclined his head. The questions leaned toward the obvious. "I have never met the gentleman but I know who he is. Penha Longa." Everyone at headquarters know who Baron Szily was. The name was high on the list of foreigners to be treated with cautious respect.

"An honored guest in our country, Inspector, and a true friend of Portugal. Baron Szily is concerned for his welfare naturally and so are we."

Machado's face lost nothing of its look of mild wonder. "Naturally, Excellency." He had no idea of what was coming, but Szily was a very rich man.

Lobo sailed ahead of the conversation as if powered by some inner certainty. "Baron Szily has an art collection that is priceless. He is leaving it to the nation."

"Another Gulbenkian." The remark tripped and fell for some reason. Machado hurried a fulsome smile.

"Someone entered Baron Szily's house this afternoon and a car was seen in the woods nearby. The owner was a certain Gunilla von Mayenfels who was once employed at Penha Longa. The name doesn't mean anything to you?"

Machado searched his memory. There was a file in his office devoted to complaints made by one foreigner against another. They denounced one another for complicated forms of immorality, downright dishonesty and subversive activities. Each complaint had to be investigated. Most were found to be a waste of time. He shook his head.

"Nothing at all, Excellency."

"Her father was a German diplomat stationed here at the end of the war."

Machado made what he hoped were the correct noises. "Is that the whole story, Excellency? A girl, a car and an intruder?"

Lobo's look was bland. "I believe that there is more. In fact I'm sure there is. Baron Szily will tell you himself. He wants no fuss. His request for help is strictly unofficial. But it is taken seriously at the highest level."

"Naturally." Machado was achieving a degree of urbanity that pleased him.

"Your instructions are simple, Inspector. Deal with this matter in whatever way the Baron wishes and report to your Minister. Do I make myself clear?"

"Almost." Machado licked his gleaming teeth. "What happens if I fail, Excellency?"

Lobo chuckled as if genuinely amused. "Then nobody wants to hear about it. I shall leave this report with you. Burn it when you have read it."

The envelope landed in Machado's lap. There was no writing on it, no name or address. The reverse side was sealed with blobs of red wax.

"The Baron expects you at Penha Longa. Seven-thirty. The gatekeeper has been told of your arrival. Above all, Inspector — *discretion*. Don't bother to see me out."

Machado stood well back from the window, watching Lobo to the limousine. It left in a shower of churned turf, the noise of the exhaust shattering the peace of the lane.

He lit a cheroot, slit the envelope and sat with his back to the window. The three photocopies inside bore the same date, June 28, 1945. Practice allowed him to scan whole paragraphs and pick out the salient points. What he read first was a memorandum from the Foreign Minister of the time to the President of the Council. A large part of Machado's life seemed to have been spent looking at these bald recitals of fact. The characters were never more than skeletons without flesh and he wondered about their hearts and guts. The memorandum dealt with the events of the night of May 7, 1945. The surrender of the Third Reich was imminent. Neighbors living in the vicinity had reported a fire in the German embassy. The fire brigade had answered the call promptly, locating the conflagration in the library. Machado smiled, bucktoothed, as the account took on comical overtones. The embassy staff had been burning secret documents and the blaze had set the curtains alight. A situation developed in which the fire brigade tried to extinguish the flames while the Germans were intent on destroying their files. A truce was called and the embassy staff had withdrawn. The surrender of the Third Reich was announced the following day. Police sealed off the embassy and placed it under strict guard. The ambassador had lodged a complaint before surrendering his credentials. The complaint was against his second secretary and security officer. Mayenfels was alleged to have vanished with a valuable collection of jeweled jade figures that had arrived from Berlin by courier. Three hours later the ambassador and the rest of his staff had crossed the frontier into Spain. There was a record of two subsequent inquiries about the missing man and property, both from representatives of the Allied governments. The Portuguese had disclaimed all knowledge of the matter and declared it officially closed.

Machado dropped the memorandum on the floor beside him. The second report was from the officer commanding the Tenth District Lisbon Volunteer Fire Brigade. It stated that his unit had responded to a call timed at twenty hours, May 7, 1945. Fires were extinguished in the library and code room of the German embassy. Nothing had been removed from the premises. Machado blew the ash from his cheroot, appreciating the indignation in the final statement.

The last report was from the Mem Martins post of the Guarda Nacional Republicano and pecked out on a non-aligned typewriter in no-nonsense prose. It described the finding of a burnt-out Mercedes sedan with diplomatic plates on the night of May 7, 1945. There were no eyewitnesses to the disaster and the vehicle was assumed to have gone out of control and hit a tree on the Sintra highway. The charred body of a man had been found inside and removed by officials of the Instituto de Medicina Legal. Examination of the corpse established that a broken neck was the immediate cause of death. The car was registered in the name of Mayenfels. Fragments of a passport bearing the same name had been found among the scorched clothing. The body had been unclaimed and buried under a plain headstone in the Mem Martins cemetery. Instructions for this had come from the high command of P.I.D.E, the security police.

Machado found his magnifying glass. The strong lens established faint pencil markings which must have showed plainly on the original. He smiled again, this time in appreciation. Latin had been hammered into his head with the assistance of hard knuckles. *Agrescit mebendo,* he read. The cure is worse than the disease. Underneath was written in Portuguese, *no further action necessary.*

Machado burned the envelope and its contents and flushed away the ashes. This was a forty-year-old scandal involving foreigners and it had taken another foreigner to revive it, a man who could pick up a phone and make an "unofficial request" that might jeopardize the hunt for someone like Kosky. His workroom, as he called it, was at the other end of the passage. Most of the things he kept there had neither beauty nor use. A plastic rattle and a silver-plated spoon bought for a child that had not lived to see them. A flattened disk of lead, the remains of a bullet that had parted Machado's shirt from his skin. A metronome that had been his mother's. Dusty seed catalogues. His father's watch chain, silver on brass, the medal attached commemorating the last king of Portugal.

He stuffed his pockets with cheroots and opened the drawer where he kept his gun. It was a five-shot revolver that had been confiscated from an American gambler thrown out of Estoril. It was beautifully balanced, with a walnut stock and a two-inch barrel. He spun the cylinder and checked the safety catch. He scribbled a note for his wife. The hours he kept were no longer a topic of conversation between them. Whenever he came home late, her vast warm body accepted his in the bed, grumbling a little about the roughness of his beard or the fact that his knees were cold. Whenever he compared other women to her, he remembered Luisa as he had first seen her, a slim girl with hair piled on her head, washing clothes in a river. A woman who loses her only child has a place apart. Neither spoke now of the tragedy but each recognized the other's gnawing hunger.

He called his office and left word that he was incommunicado for the next two hours. His next call was to the Hotel Mondial where he asked for Senhor Martins. Cabral came on the line.

"Our friend is still in his room. He ate something but he's had no visitors. I'm staying close."

"Good," said Machado. "I'm going out on a job for the Scavengers." It was police slang for the Inspectors of Cause. "It sounds to me like one of their more extravagant inventions but I'll know more when I've seen the man concerned. In any case our plans are the same. I'll meet you at nine." He gave the name of a big, bustling place serving shellfish and beer.

He relinquished the phone, wondering about Szily. Obviously Lobo knew more than he'd said, which was typical. No matter how much you credited the Scavengers with knowing, they always knew more. He let himself out and pointed the small Renault up into the hills. The sun had set beyond Queluz leaving the rocks and bush still bathed in violet twilight. The road to Penha Longa sloped down, picking up a high boundary wall on the left. Opposite was a dense cork-oak forest. Machado stopped in front of imposing gilded gates. A man dressed in olive-green livery hurried out and let the Renault through. Machado wound down his window, observing the customary courtesies.

"Good evening, Senhor. My name is Machado. I have an appointment with Baron Szily."

The gatekeeper edged a little closer. "If the Senhor permits . . ."

Machado waved permission. "By all means."

The man's crumpled Moorish face grew sly. "The Senhor is from the authorities?"

"Speak," said Machado.

The gatekeeper cleared his throat, looking around conspiratorially. "I am the one who saw her car," he announced in a hoarse whisper. "The German woman. It was over there in the trees." He described an arc with his arm.

Machado looked him up and down. "What were you doing on government property?"

The man's face fell. "With all respect, Senhor. I do what I am paid to do. I keep my eyes open."

"You can get something in them that way," said Machado. "And the open mouth catches flies! What is that confounded noise?"

"The dogs, Senhor. They are usually loose at this hour but tonight the Senhor Baron has given instructions."

Machado let the clutch out. A grove of eucalyptus trees bordered the graveled driveway while on the right cropped grass stretched away into long purple shadows. The baying of the dogs grew louder as he drove past glowing windows and stopped on a sweep of asphalt in front of the house. Stone bears under the massive porch stood on each side of the great dark door. Machado wiped his face and hands on his handkerchief, reversed it and tucked it so that the clean ends showed in his pocket. He put his hat squarely on his head, walked across to the door and pulled a bell handle. Lights came on in the hall. A middle-aged woman with flat gray hair parted in the center opened the door. She was wearing a lace-edged apron over her black uniform. She stood to one side, smiling politely.

"The Senhor Baron is waiting in the library. If the Senhor will come this way?"

Machado surrendered his hat. The stone walls were hung with grinning fox masks and the antlered heads of deer. He traced the sweet unfamiliar fragrance to some bowls containing dried flower petals and reminded himself to tell Luisa about them. He followed the maid along a corridor lined with gilt-and-plaster figures to a door. The maid tapped on it gently.

"The gentleman, Senhor Baron!"

An elderly man dressed in a frogged velvet smoking jacket rose from a table littered with newspapers. His hair was almost colorless. The backs of his hands and the pouches of skin under his jaw were mottled with mustard-colored stains. His Portuguese was grammatically perfect, and strongly accented.

"I am happy to make your acquaintance, Inspector. I hope you have not been too much inconvenienced."

There was a natural assumption of authority, a basic indifference to Machado's inconvenience that was instantly recognizable. Machado played the game according to the rules.

"Always at your orders, Excellency."

His eyes took in the room. Everything had the bloom of

wealth. Tapestry, gilt-and-leather books on the shelves, a gold-handled paper knife. His guess was that it would have taken him a year's salary to pay for the carpet.

Szily indicated a chair. "Please make yourself comfortable. I understand that you are something of an expert on conspiracy." His own chair was straight-backed and he sat it as if in a saddle.

Machado rolled his eyeballs modestly. "Your Excellency flatters me."

"So," said Szily. "The courtesies disposed of, let's get down to business. You know why you are here?"

Machado's gesture excused his ignorance. "Not completely, Senhor Baron. A car was seen in the woods nearby. The owner was a woman who worked for you. And that is the extent of my information. I understood that you would be explaining more fully."

Szily's gaze was Baltic-bleak. "I have a well-trained staff, Inspector, and I encourage them to believe that my interests are theirs. My gatekeeper saw this car in the state forest and recognized it. Naturally he informed me. Now if Miss Mayenfels chooses to trespass, that is her affair. But I have reason to believe that she was doing far more than that. An intruder was in my house this afternoon. In this very room. The tapestry you see covers a door that leads to my private museum. Whoever was here must have been examining it."

The parrot whistled loudly, the sound vanishing along the corridor. Machado had an impression of a house where servants tiptoed past open doors, of silence where people sat and waited. Wealth combined with privilege made an island of this place, an island that was immune to invasion, or supposedly. He was careful to hide his skepticism with a show of deference.

"Your theory is that Miss Mayenfels was the intruder?"

Szily fanned the air. "It's not just my theory. She was seen later driving with a man twelve kilometers away. You see, Inspector, the people in the neighborhood know her by sight and country people are observant. They say that the man looked like a foreigner."

Machado licked his lips and started again.

"With respect, Senhor Baron. A man with a hoe considers a man from the city a foreigner."

Szily leaned back, his penetrating gaze very blue and bright. "I agree. But this was no man with a hoe. It was the wife of our local doctor. She saw the Mayenfels girl and called my secretary to find out if Gunilla was back here working. These people have little to do in the wintertime, little to occupy their minds."

Machado touched his handkerchief to his lips with great delicacy. "But is Your Excellency certain that an intruder was actually *in* the house?"

Szily reached under the table. A section of one of the legs swung out under his touch. By craning forward, Machado could see a small built-in unit with photoelectric cells and a tiny clock face. Szily pointed at what looked like a curtain fixture on the outside wall.

"That is my invisible watchdog. Anyone approaching the museum door is obliged to pass through the beam. You'll see that there are three positions. Off, On and Register. If I set the mechanism thus, in the second position, an alarm rings in my bedroom when the beam is broken. The third position is slightly more sophisticated. No alarm sounds but the time of the intrusion is registered here." He tapped the face of the clock. The hands showed 5:37.

Machado blinked. "Could it not have been a servant?"

Szily folded the unit back into the table leg. He answered with absolute certainty.

"This room is cleaned every morning while I am riding horseback. None of the staff comes in here again until the following day. As I told you, my people are well-trained."

Machado eased himself into a more comfortable position. "My instructions are to obey your orders, Senhor Baron. You had better tell me what you wish me to do."

Szily's teeth were the products of an expensive dentist and he was confident of them. He lifted a fold of the tapestry and rapped on the steel behind with his knuckles.

"Behind this door is everything that I care about in life, Inspector. I have made my home here for forty years and I'm grateful to your country. I have no heirs. When I die, everything I own, including the contents of my museum, goes to Portugal."

Machado shifted his legs. "Portugal is honored."

Szily's tone put lemon back in the honeyed exchange. "But in the meantime I demand something in return. I demand to be allowed to enjoy my possessions for as long as I live."

"Naturally." Machado's voice was cautious.

"I believe that an attempt is going to be made to steal my treasures. Not only that, I believe that the thieves are abetted by Gunilla von Mayenfels. I intend to deal with this outrage in my own way."

Machado worried the end of his nose. "A car in the

woods? An intrusion? It is little enough to go on, Excellency."

Szily went through the objection at the gallop. "What do you want, masked men bursting in with pistols? I don't think you understand, Inspector. This is a cunningly devised scheme to rob me. This woman is consorting with professional thieves. But I intend to trap them."

"Trap them?" Machado blinked.

Szily made a vice of his hand and closed it. "Like that. My opinion is that these thieves are almost surely foreigners. Portugal doesn't produce such viciousness."

Machado came out of his daydream. "You are probably right. Foreigners who know exactly what they are looking for. A painting ripped from its frame would be easily concealed."

" 'Ripped from its frame,' " Szily repeated, wincing. "Have you any idea what it means to me to hear you say that? To think of vandals handling priceless works of art?"

Machado jerked his head. "I've seen burgled houses, Excellency. I know how people feel."

Szily lifted a bony hand. "Gunilla Mayenfels catalogued my museum, remember! Any one of a dozen paintings in my collection would fit in a dispatch case and we all know there are unscrupulous men who buy such things without question. Corots, Vermeers."

Machado sneaked a look at his watch, making a show of interest at the same time in case Szily noticed.

"I can have this woman under lock and key in a matter of minutes. These people always talk, Excellency. There are enough witnesses. Then you can sleep untroubled."

Szily came to his feet and walked to the parrot's perch. "I have a different idea, Inspector. I told you, I intend to deal with these people in my own way."

Machado looked across the room cautiously. "Would you explain what that means, Senhor Baron?"

The parrot lay in Szily's hands upside down as if dead. He blew softly into its feathers.

"I shall make things easy for them. As I said, *trap* them. This is my house and I have the right to defend it." He placed the bird back on its perch. It squawked and shuffled away.

Machado's teeth protruded through a nervous smile. "You place me in a difficult position. These thieves may well be armed and I am personally responsible for your safety."

"I absolve you of that responsibility," Szily said calmly. "Contact your superiors if you are still worried. I've had a room prepared for you in the guesthouse. I want you to sleep there till this affair has been brought to a conclusion. There are able-bodied men we can count on. I want no more police on my property."

"Then why do you *want* me here?" demanded Machado. "Your Excellency speaks of defending your property, able-bodied men and the rest. What is my part in all this?"

"You are the representative of law and order," said Szily.

Machado raised his arms and let them fall again. "Do you know my post and rank, Senhor Baron?"

Szily smiled. "And your record. It gives me confidence. There might be things that you have to do in Lisbon, Inspector. Matters you can't deal with by telephone. I shall expect you back by eleven."

Machado brought his feet together and bowed from the neck. "Eleven o'clock, Excellency, and many thanks."

Szily skipped on patent-leather pumps. He touched Machado's shoulder in comradely fashion.

"You'll see, Inspector. I have a surprise waiting for them."

Crazy, thought Machado. Drunk with riches and power and crazy. He settled himself behind the wheel of the Renault, lifting a hand in response to Szily's farewell. The gatekeeper let him out, his grinning Moorish face yellow in the lamplight. He was carrying a double-barreled shotgun under his arm with the safety catches off.

"A good journey, Senhor. If God wishes."

Machado put his foot down hard. He seemed to find an extra sense at night, driving with speed and certainty as the Renault snaked down the country roads behind dipped headlights. It was almost nine when Machado parked by the castle, five minutes later by the time he reached the *cervejaria*. The massive marble counter was piled with mussels, crabs and clams. Waiters in wet aprons were netting lobsters from the tanks, scuffling through the sawdust carrying schooners of beer. Machado threaded his way through the deafening noise to a corner table. He took the spare chair, drank an inch of beer from Cabral's glass and flicked his fingers for the waiter.

"You lost him," he said without ceremony.

Cabral was hatless and wearing a light tan coat around his shoulders like a cloak.

"Wrong. I didn't lose him."

Machado scrambled a cheroot from his pocket to his mouth, scanning the surrounding tables. It was a place that was popular with businessmen and bullfight *aficionados*. He could see no one he knew.

"So?"

Cabral winked. The rest of his face remained expressionless. "He left the hotel just after seven and walked toward Chiado. Make no mistake, this one knows every dodge in the book. In one door and out the other, back-doubling, using parked cars as mirrors."

A waiter bustled up. Machado ordered more beer and a plate of prawns. Cabral stayed silent till the man had come and gone.

"But I'm just as smart as he is. I stayed with him as far as a bar near here and hung around in the building opposite. I could see right into the place. Someone was waiting for Kosky. It was obvious that the man knew him from the way they greeted one another. The man was elderly, fat and well-dressed, a foreigner by his appearance. They talked for a while then this man gave Kosky an envelope."

Machado picked the thread of offal from the spine of a prawn and closed his teeth on the salty flesh. He spoke with his mouth full.

"Did you see what was in the envelope?"

Cabral shook his head. "A woman came into the building and I had to move. But it looked as if Kosky was counting."

Machado spit a shred of shell at the sawdust. "Money, probably."

Cabral tilted back on his chair. "Two more people arrived, a man and a woman. The man was in his thirties, the woman a few years younger. There was more talk and another envelope changed hands. They broke up almost immediately. Kosky went left, the fat man right. The girl and the other man were driving a green Volkswagen. I already knew where to get hold of Kosky so I followed the others in a cab."

"You did well." Machado pushed the plate of prawns across to Cabral and lit a cheroot. A strange fancy had started to bubble in his brain. "This man you followed, the one in the Volkswagen, did he look like a foreigner too?"

"He *is* a foreigner. The girl drove him to the Carlton Hotel. Here's the entry in the register." He passed a slip across the table.

Machado stared down at it. "And he arrived today?"

"On the T.A.P. flight from London. I can tell you the name of the girl as well. I checked the numbers of the car with the Transit Police."

The bubble exploded an Machado held up a hand. "I *know* who she is. Her name is Gunilla von Mayenfels, a German national born in this country. Right or wrong?"

"Right," said Cabral. His face rarely expressed emotion but now it was frankly curious. "Do you want to tell me how you know?"

Machado told him. Cabral listened with his head sunk between his hands. The coat had slipped unnoticed from his shoulders.

"Caramba!" he said when Machado had finished.

Machado took the cheroot from his mouth and studied it gravely. "I am getting old, Luis, and I need ideas."

Cabral took his hands away from his face. "The day is to come when you need ideas. You're as wily as a fox. All you need is a sounding board, but nevertheless I think that what we have here are two distinct operations. We'll call the first one the Mayenfels syndrome, a planned assault on Szily's treasures with the help of a professional thief. The second is Kosky's participation and this one defeats me. I can't quite make up my mind how he fits in."

Machado pushed himself up from the table. "I'll be back in a couple of minutes."

The pay phones were near the cloakroom. He fed a coin into the slot, dialed his office and tapped the box nervously. It could well be one of Pacheco's roller-skating evenings. The woolly, spinsterish voice set his mind at rest. Machado read from Cabral's slip of paper.

"Make a note. Scott Hamilton, Canadian subject, passport issued in Ottawa, number 836521. Get a Telex off to Scotland Yard, Urgent and Top Priority. Ask for anything known about this man and remember that it has to go through Interpol. Next query, a woman called Gunilla von Mayenfels, a German with a Resident's Visa. There'll be something on her downstairs in Records. Just grab it and sign. Give no reasons to anyone."

Pacheco's excitement was giving him trouble. "The cards, Senhor Cabo. The aliens' cards! This Hamilton was one of the names I . . . "

"Get off the line and do as you're told," bawled Machado. He lowered his voice. "As soon as you can, Pacheco." He mashed the receiver down and wiped his neck with his handkerchief.

He was wearing his sly chipmunk face when he returned to the table. "We'll see what London says about this Hamilton. I'm checking the girl out with Records."

Cabral was cleaning his fingers with a slice of lemon. "I've been thinking. We're assuming that Hamilton's a professional, right?"

"Right. Known to the police or not, he has to be."

Cabral cocked his long dark head. "Then we know more about Kosky than he does. No professional thief is going to associate with someone like Kosky if he knows who he really is."

Machado relit the dead cheroot in the ashtray. "Tell me why a gang of art thieves needs a private inquiry agent traveling on a French passport, a man speaking Portuguese with a Brazilian accent!"

Cabral's elbows thudded softly on the table. He leaned forward, eyes narrowed and brilliant.

"I can't do that but I can tell you why Kosky needs *them*." He rubbed his left thumb and forefinger together. "Funds for the party. You mentioned a Corot, a Vermeer. Either of those is worth millions of escudos. Kosky's going to double-cross his partners. I feel it here." He tapped the side of his head.

Machado put some money on the table and smiled approvingly. "For a man with a degree in law, you show a lot of common sense. You realize what this means, if we play our cards right?"

Cabral nodded. "Communist agent taken red-handed in an attempt to steal the nation's heritage. It's as good as a bomb up his ass. He should have stayed in France."

Machado beckoned his partner closer. He could see the gold at the back of Cabral's mouth.

"We have a problem on our hands. Szily. The man's daft enough to spoil everything. We'll tell him no more than is good for him. I'll have to get you into the house somehow."

Cabral draped his coat around his shoulders. "When do you think they'll make their move?"

Machado turned the corners of his mouth down. "Who knows? You take the Mondial, I'll take the Carlton."

They crossed the street and walked up between the staggered lamps. Old buildings stood on each other's heads, scabs of plaster peeling from their façades. There was a smell of fried squid and urine and the cobbled passages shone in the yellow light with the accumulated grease of centuries. The two climbed narrow streets that flew down like roller-coaster chutes, past taverns oozing melancholy evocative music. Machado grunted.

Cabral smiled. "Why is it that you don't like fado?"

The Renault was high on the hill where the castle of St. George dominated the wide river. Machado opened the doors.

"Because it's Moorish and not Portuguese. Women in shawls singing 'shalalala' through their noses."

Cabral slid in beside him. "You have no soul, that's your trouble."

Machado's breath was short from the climb. He touched himself between the legs.

"This is where my soul is. If Kosky isn't in the hotel, just stay there. I'll call you back in half an hour."

He put the Renault in motion, driving it down the narrow street like a bobsled, one hand pressing on the horn-ring. He stopped on Rossio. The immense square was blocked with cars, flower sellers were still doing business and the sidewalk cafés were crowded. Cabral unlocked his long legs.

"Thanks for the lift. We still don't know who the fat man is."

Machado lowered his window, beckoning a boy from the pavement. He exchanged a coin for an afternoon paper. A thousand cars seemed to blare in unison from the direction of the Avenida da Liberdade.

"We don't need to know," he answered, staring at the smudged photograph on the front page. "The others will tell us."

He watched Cabral to the north end of the square and joined the whirlpool of traffic. He made a left at the third set of signals and coasted into a no-parking area. He pressed the rubber sucker of his V.I.P. disk against the windshield and walked up the steps to the hotel. People were going into the restaurant. The chairs and sofas in the lobby were practically deserted. He made his way to the reception desk, leaned across and beckoned the clerk over. He spoke urgently and in a low voice. The clerk's expression changed from urbanity to guarded apprehension.

"But there was another gentleman here from the police earlier. I hope this isn't going to mean trouble."

"Do as you're told," ordered Machado.

The clerk nodded hurriedly. "*Si,* Senhor." He ran his finger down a room list and picked up the telephone. "Sorry to have troubled you, sir," he said in English. "I have the wrong room." He put the phone down, his eyes on Machado's face. "He's in."

Machado glanced around the lobby. "How many ways are there out of this place?"

"Only one, sir." The clerk nodded at the front entrance.

"Very well, listen carefully. I'm going to sit over there where you can see me. If this man comes down you will signal me, so — with your head — but discreetly."

The clerk's face had gone completely bloodless. "I think perhaps, with the Senhor's permission, the manager . . ."

Machado stood on his toes and leaned over the counter. "Shit in the manager's hat, my friend. And if you don't do exactly as you are told, neither you nor the manager will be working here much longer."

He made his way to an empty sofa and sank down, his face almost hidden behind the newspaper. He looked at the front page for the tenth time. A black terrorist had just been fêted in Stockholm. The agency picture portrayed him arriving at the airport, grinning into the camera, fist clenched, surrounded by earnest white faces. Machado's sense of indignation was strong. There was no limit to the infamy of these people. They were living out a death wish and trying to take others with them. Their children collected money to support people like Kosky whose avowed aim was to destroy Western civilization. The minutes stretched, fifteen, then thirty. He walked to a booth and called the Mondial Hotel. Cabral came on the line.

"Kosky's in bed and asleep," he said curtly. "He left a call for eight in the morning. There's no way out unless the bastard can fly."

"Stay where you are till I call again. I'm waiting for the other one to appear. Ring Pacheco and see what he has on the girl."

He crossed to the desk again and rapped sharply on the counter. The clerk's face was green under the shaded lamp. He drew himself up wearily.

"How many calls have been made from that room?" demanded Machado.

The clerk's hands were expressive. "How can I answer, Senhor? Calls are recorded at the switchboard, not here."

"Then get them," snapped Machado. "I want names and numbers, every one."

The clerk disappeared through a door. He was back again in a couple of minutes, his face anxious.

"Just the two calls, Senhor. One to the Global Travel Agency, the other to a Senhor Kohn at the Ritz Hotel."

The fat man certainly. Machado scribbled the names and numbers on a piece of paper.

"Much better," he said. "Now we're beginning to understand one another."

The clerk's expression altered abruptly. The words came in a rapid mumble.

"The elevator, Senhor! The tall man on the left. Senhor Hamilton!" He shot back to his desk and buried his head in the papers there.

Machado turned around slowly. The group of people emerging from the elevator was already halfway across the lobby. A couple of American matrons with mauve rinses and harlequin spectacles were accompanied by a well-fed escort in a drip-dry suit. The three of them bore down on the desk with all the confidence of tourists bent on seeing the town. Machado moved out of their way, his eyes on the man walking toward the bar. The Canadian walked with a bounce, his shoulders swinging slightly. Longish graying hair covered the collar of his blue flannel jacket. Machado went into the bar after him and made himself inconspicuous in a corner. Hamilton was on a stool, talking to the bartender. Machado could see that the Canadian's nose had been flattened across the bridge, giving him a combative look as he smiled, looking up at the bottles. The bartender reached for a glass. Hamilton swung around on his stool, looking the room over. His gaze flicked past Machado disinterestedly and settled on the couple at the next table. Machado appreciated his choice. The slim, dark-haired girl had the *panache* of the well-bred South American, beautiful, desirable and completely unapproachable. The youngster with her said something in Spanish. They both stared briefly at Hamilton and laughed. He completed his inspection of the tables very deliberately and turned his back.

Machado picked a handful of nuts from the bowl in front of him. A waiter hovered expectantly. Machado asked for beer.

"Danish, German or Dutch, Senhor?"

"This is Portugal," Machado reminded curtly.

The waiter's eyes wavered. "I am sorry, Senhor. We do not serve Portuguese beer."

Machado shook his head, cleaning the fragments of nut from his teeth with his tongue.

"A glass of port wine, then."

He scowled at the check on the table, feeling in his pockets for change. American films, English television and

Danish beer. It was a miracle that his countrymen still spoke their own language. The bar had started to fill with people coming from the restaurant, more foreigners, stuffed with food and noisy with drink. They were always so very sure of their welcome. The Canadian suddenly slid from his stool and walked out to the lobby. The elevator gates were already closing as Machado reached the door. He watched the blinking lights. Hamilton had stopped on the second floor. Machado stepped into a phone booth and called Cabral.

"Get up to headquarters as soon as you can."

He walked over to the reception desk and rapped on the counter. The clerk came out of his chair, licking his lips.

"What's your name?" Machado demanded.

"Duarte, Senhor Inspector. José Saramento Duarte."

Machado made a show of noting it on a slip of paper. He leaned forward, his bulging eyes uncharacteristically ferocious.

"You are on probation, Senhor Duarte. One word of any of this to your colleagues, even to the manager, and you are in bad, bad trouble. Do you understand?"

Duarte's composure had been completely wrecked. "I am a family man, Senhor, a good Catholic, and I obey the law. The Inspector can rely on me."

"The Inspector hopes so. Good night, Senhor Duarte."

He took the sticker from the windshield of the Renault and put it back in the glove compartment. It was almost ten as he drove up Chiado and down Rua Antonio Maria Cardoso. Banks of indigo cloud were building up beneath a sliver of moon over the Atlantic. He jammed the Renault hard up against the wall and walked into the building. Women with mops and pails were washing the stone-flagged entrance hall. He hurried along the deserted corridors and up the stone flight of stairs. A light showed under the door of Pacheco's office. He pressed the button on his desk and his aide came in, his acne-pitted face tense and excited.

"The girl's file is on your desk, Senhor Cabo. I told Inspector Cabral when he phoned."

Machado snapped on the lamp. A small green folder was in the middle of his blotter.

"No reply to the Telex yet?"

There were fresh food stains on the front of Pacheco's jacket. "No, Senhor. But it went ten minutes after you spoke to me. Communications marked it Urgent."

Machado grunted. "If the police in England are not on strike we should hear something by morning. Let's see what their iron brain does for us." His faith in computers was limited.

"*Si,* Senhor Cabo." Pacheco's voice sounded tired.

"Have you eaten?" Machado asked suddenly.

"A sandwich, Senhor. B Squad is up in the dormitory. They gave me coffee."

Machado had fought hard for the two rooms at the top of the building. He had fitted them out with bunks and washbasins. Squads on standby duty used them as rest rooms.

"Go home and get some sleep," Machado said kindly. "You've had a long day."

Pacheco hesitated. "I could sleep upstairs. You might need me."

"You'll sleep in your bed and that's an order," Machado answered. "Good night!"

He heard Pacheco in the next room putting his desk in order and pulling up the blinds. Every drawer would be locked before he left, the confidential papers put away in the big safe. Pacheco would remember his duties on his deathbed. Machado hung his hat on the back of the door and sat down at the desk. The operational strength of Centrintel was no more than fifty men, eight teams of five with two back-up squads. He had kept the numbers purposely low. Each man had been hand-picked from the rush of volunteers that had answered his appeal. He knew their virtues and failings, their families. His men's loyalty to him was as absolute as his to them.

He shuffled through the pile of alien-registration cards till he found the one he was looking for. It bore the stamp of the Ritz Hotel.

KOHN, Philip. British. Aged 69. Antique-dealer.

He groped for the tattered package in his pocket. The frayed end of a cheroot flared in the flame. He shut his right eye, avoiding the stream of smoke, staring down at the card. *Antique-dealer!* They operated with effrontery, these people, conducting their business almost at the scene of the crime. He opened the file Pacheco had brought up from Records. It contained the same old array of names, dates and places. Facts, without a single original thought.

VON MAYENFELS, Gunilla Margret, born Estoril, February 28, 1944; ward of Utte Taube, deceased. Attended state schools and the Carmelite convent in Benfica. German passport issued in 1959, attended school in England. Work-permit issued in 1963. Present employment, secretary-translator, Alpha Engineering S.A., Travessa do Sr. Prior, Lisbon 1. Civil status, spinster. Home address, 18 Miguel Bombarda, Praia de Pera.

He shut the folder as Cabral came in, still wearing his fawn coat like a cloak. Machado uncovered his rabbit's teeth.

"Well, I had a good look at our Canadian friend."

Cabral lolled on the horsehair sofa, stroking an ankle. "And?"

Machado shrugged. "Long hair like an actor. Dresses well, almost as well as you, in fact. He smiles a great deal and feels very sure of himself."

"Maybe he has good reason. You mean you left him there alone in the hotel?"

"In his room," said Machado.

Cabral nodded. "He could be on his way to Penha Longa at this very moment. Suppose Kosky isn't actually needed on the job."

Machado's face was calm. "We'll suppose nothing of the sort." He searched for an unused fold in his handkerchief and spit carefully into it. "Kosky moves when Hamilton does."

Cabral lifted his gloved hand. "How about his room? He's bound to leave it sometime. We could have it searched."

Machado upturned the ashtray into the cuspidor. "And discover what? A weapon, burglary tools? These are the things we expect him to have. No, Luis, what we do here is to leave them all alone and remember that the big cards are ours. All we have to do is play them correctly. Listen to this."

He read from Kohn's card. "Hamilton phoned him this evening. There's your fat man. He is an antique-dealer. See how it all fits in?"

Cabral's smile was mocking. "You mean he's paid in advance for his painting? Then he's out of his mind. Kosky will run rings around both of them."

"But not around us," Machado said firmly. "Let's go upstairs and brief the men."

V

MACHADO WAKED to the sound of trotting horses and shuffled to the window in borrowed silk pajamas that were a couple of sizes too big for him. The guesthouse stood on a knoll surrounded by clipped yew hedges wet from the spray of a garden hose and brilliant in the early sunshine. The ring of hoofs was louder as the horses moved onto the cobblestones. He could see the two horsemen, Szily ahead on an iron-gray Lusitano stallion, the stocky groom a couple of lengths behind, mounted on a chestnut.

The two men disappeared in the direction of the eucalyptus grove. Machado let the curtain fall with reluctant admiration. The clock on the bedside table showed quarter-after-seven. It had been three before Szily had agreed to go to bed, yet there he was, sitting up like a troop sergeant.

Machado scratched himself vigorously, looking around the room. There were no blankets on the bed. He had slept as Szily assured him the Germans did, under a linen sheet buttoned to an eiderdown quilt. The dark massive furniture was lustrous with wax and care. There was everything that a guest might need. Fruit, cigarettes, a bottle of mineral water, a selection of books, a new razor and toothbrush in the luxuriously fitted bathroom. He showered and shaved. Breakfast was served in the big house at eight-thirty. The dogs were barking as he made his way down the path into the rose garden.

A man looked up as Machado passed, his face already shining with sweat. The servants at Penha Longa were shyly courteous as if wholly unused to visitors. The massive front doors at the head of the steps stood wide open to the sunshine. The gleaming hall smelled of beeswax and the fragrance of potpourri. The middle-aged maid he had seen the night before came forward to greet him. She was wearing a gray poplin uniform with a cap of the same material. She smiled.

"*Bom dia,* Senhor! If the Senhor will come this way?"

She led him through the corridor to the patio. The sun warmed the bougainvilleas. A trolley was laden with breakfast things, a heavy silver coffeepot, silver chafing dishes. The parrot was mumbling a piece of cuttlefish bone on its perch at the far end of the patio. The maid smiled again.

"No more than a tiny moment! The Senhor Baron is never late for meals."

She nodded encouragingly and closed the door behind her. Seconds later a clock sounded in the distance. Eight-thirty. The drone of carpet sweepers and floor polishers stopped abruptly. The house was completely silent. The heavy tread of riding boots sounded in the corridor and Szily came in. Exercise had reddened his leathery face. He was wearing a black polo shirt and stained whipcord breeches. He walked across to the parrot and scratched the bird's poll, looking at Machado.

"You slept well, I trust?"

"Better than in my own bed," Machado answered truthfully.

Szily's smile was frugal. "A dangerous precedent." He lifted the covers on the chafing dishes and inspected the contents. "Please sit down."

Machado considered the grapefruit in front of him. These foreigners ate the wrong way around.

"A fine horse," he ventured politely.

Szily cocked an eyebrow. "How much do you know about horses, Inspector?"

Machado spooned sugar over the grapefruit as Szily had done. "Nothing."

Szily's tone reflected the intimacy they had established the previous night. "I find your candor refreshing, Inspector. Now I'd like you to be equally honest about something else. Do you still resent my refusal to allow more police on my property?"

Machado found the grapefruit bitter in spite of the sugar. He pushed the plate to one side and helped himself to sausages, bacon and eggs.

" 'Resent' is too strong a word, Senhor Baron. I'm disappointed that you won't make an exception for Inspector Cabral. He's a highly efficient officer."

"So are you." Szily buttered a slice of toast, ignoring the side dishes. "I'm tremendously impressed at the way you're handling this case. To locate and identify these thieves in a few short hours is quite an achievement. It gives me a feeling of security."

The unexpectedness of Machado's belch took him by surprise. It worried him that Szily might think him ill-mannered. The thought put him on the defensive.

"If security matters so much to you, why ask for police assistance and then not use it? To me this makes no sense."

Szily ate on one side of his mouth as if the other were reserved for a different purpose.

"Obviously. Since this is the fifth time you have referred to it, Inspector."

"And I still don't understand," Machado said obstinately.

"It's the question of your responsibility, isn't it? You feel that if something went wrong, then the blame would be yours. Isn't that your principal worry?"

"Partly," Machado admitted.

Szily put his cup down very deliberately. "Imagine an attack has been made on your wife. Your first concern is for her safety. But there are other reactions, surely. Indignation and rage. You'd feel like taking her assailant by the throat before you handed him over to justice."

Machado shook his head. "A false analogy, if you'll allow me to say so. My wife is neither a Corot nor a Vermeer. My belief is that this plan of yours, this *trap,* as you call it, could endanger your life. There isn't a painting in the world that is worth it."

Szily pushed the coffeepot across the table. "Wrong, Inspector. What's in my museum is the expression of man's noblest aspirations, beauty that should be permanent. But my enjoyment of these things is only temporary. That's why I demand that it be complete. You could describe it as a poignant love, in no way inferior to the love that a man may have for a woman."

Machado held up his hand. "I know when I'm beaten, Excellency. Now if you'll excuse me . . . "

"There are things that you must do in Lisbon," Szily put in, his white eyebrows quizzical. He pulled a fob watch from his breeches and consulted it. "One of these days I must come to headquarters. Tell me, do they still use the *oubliettes?*"

Machado nodded, his face straight. "And the thumbscrews and racks."

Szily tugged at the top of a riding boot. "Have you made up your mind where you will station your men?"

"Yes," said Machado. What he really wanted to say was that in spite of obstacles put in his way he was still an efficient policeman. He named a hamlet commanding the crossroads five kilometers away.

"I know someone there, an old school friend, a veterinarian."

"You think the attempt will be made tonight?"

Machado moved a shoulder. "The signs are that it should be. If not, we just sit and wait."

Szily considered his watch again and smiled bleakly. "It's nine o'clock; even a Minister should be up by now." He took the phone from the trolley and dialed.

There was a rapid exchange between Szily and someone else, then the phone was passed to Machado. The Minister of Justice's voice was affable.

"Good morning, Machado. I hear that you're making excellent progress. Congratulations."

"At your orders," Machado said stiffly. There was surely more to come than that.

There was. The Minister's tone changed to one of reason. "I understand that you're still worried about your official position in this matter?"

"No, Excellency," Machado said stiffly. "My instructions are quite clear. And so I hope is my official position. I do whatever the Baron wishes."

"Excellent. And once again, congratulations."

Machado handed the phone back to Szily who cradled it, his gaze ironical.

Machado held his hands wide, palms upturned. "You win, Excellency! But then you always would." His smile held no malice.

"Nobody wins or loses," said Szily. "You and I are associates."

Machado finished his coffee. Kosky the tourist was no use to him. The man's true identity had to be kept secret until he was established as a despoiler of national heritage. A whisper abroad that the Butterfly Bomber was among them, the killer of police colonels, and all the *altas personalidades* would be running around like headless chickens. Conflicting orders would be flying as thick as bats and as welcome.

He finished his coffee. "I must go, Excellency."

The Baron fed the parrot a lump of sugar. "I'd like you to meet my groom when you return. He served two years with the paratroopers in Moçambique. I've put him in charge of the outside operations."

Machado smiled absently. "Of course. Then goodbye."

The gatekeeper flourished his shotgun as Machado drove up. The inspector poked his head out of the window.

"It is nine o'clock in the morning. What exactly are you supposed to be doing with that thing?"

The man unlocked the gates. "Frederico's instructions, Senhor."

"Who is Frederico?"

"The groom, Senhor. He was a sergeant like me."

Machado shook his head. Grown men playing soldiers and convinced by their roles.

"Put that weapon in the lodge and tell Frederico that I said so."

It would have taken a regiment to seal off Penha Longa and the surrounding woods. He had done his best with the means at his disposal. The two police cars could be at the house within minutes. Quatros Puntos was a huddle of buildings on the side of a rocky hill overlooking the crossroads. Machado turned his car up the one street. The big yellow house at the top was the only building in the hamlet with power and a telephone. The sagging lines hung over the whitewashed shacks below. An old woman with her head wrapped in a shawl was drawing water from a well. Hens scratched by the roadside. Pigs tied by the leg were rooting through piles of garbage. It was all much like the village where he had been born. There was the same impression of poverty borne with dignity.

The shutters of the yellow house were closed. A slab-sided shed adjoining was lighted by a single grimy barred window. Machado braked and climbed out. Saramento had always exaggerated. Top of his class at agricultural college, he might have been treating the pampered animals of the rich Lisbonese. Instead of that, he lived here alone, on call night and day, delivering scrawny cows and doctoring broken-down mules. There was no sign of the battered Land-Rover. His friend was off on his rounds. The front door was open. Machado stepped into a hallway with bare, scrubbed floorboards. The only furniture was a wicker table, bearing a telephone. The whitewashed wall behind was covered with scribbled numbers. He went through to the kitchen. A fat cat with torn ears was dozing in front of the old-fashioned wood range. Surgical instruments lay in a pan in the sink. Machado picked his way toward the police car parked in the yard outside, avoiding the iridescent pools of water. There was a strong smell of carbolic acid. A couple of buzzard hawks were feeding on something obscene fifty meters away.

Cabral was standing just outside the entrance to the shed, looking like a bishop who finds himself in a whorehouse. He was wearing a silk scarf at his neck, a pigskin jacket and dark-gray flannel trousers. Machado lifted an arm in his hail-and-farewell salute. He had seen it in an old newsreel clip featuring Mussolini and admired the gesture. It showed respect and was the shortest distance between two points.

"Good morning. Last night I slept in silk," he announced.

Cabral returned the salute. "I've been standing here for the last half-hour. What in God's name is this terrible stink?"

Machado sniffed energetically, glancing down at the runnels in the tiled floor of the shed.

"Blood," he announced with relish. "An animal has been put to death." He nodded at the contraption in the center of the shed. It looked like the parallel bars used by gymnasts but with a grim array of straps and chains.

Cabral stepped away hastily. "Jesus God," he said with feeling.

"Death comes to us all," Machado said sententiously. "What are you doing out here anyway? There's no one in the house."

Cabral stepped around a noisome puddle. "The man's your friend, not mine. Here's your answer from London. It arrived just before I left headquarters."

Machado took the envelope. "Let's see if we can find Saramento's coffee."

The cat leaped into Cabral's lap. He kneaded its fur as Machado read the Telex message.

RE YOUR ENQUIRY SCOTT HAMILTON CANADIAN NATIONAL STOP SUBJECT CONVICTED OF LARCENY CENTRAL CRIMINAL COURT HERE FEBRUARY 9 1971 STOP CHARGE LARCENY OF EMERALD NECKLACE AND BRACELET STOP SENTENCED THREE YEARS IMPRISONMENT RELEASED FEBRUARY 8 1974 STOP NO HOLDS OR

WARRANTS OUTSTANDING STOP CLASSIFIED HERE AS TRAVELING THIEF STOP REQUEST INFORMATION YOUR DISPOSITION

Machado grunted. "Your English is better than mine. Does that say that this man left prison only two days ago?"

"That's what it says." Cabral's fingers poked deeper into the cat's ruff. "He doesn't seem to waste any time."

Machado stuffed the message in his pocket. He opened an enormous larder, clucking as he saw the smoked ham hanging from the rafters, the barrels of wine and bins of potatoes and beans.

"He's probably paid in kind. Can you understand how a man can live this way, Luis?"

Cabral nodded. "Easily."

Machado was unconvinced. "My mother always said that Saramento had an inquiring mind. She taught him to read and write. Is all *this* a sign of an inquiring mind?"

Cabral tipped the cat from his lap and brushed his trousers. "Kohn spent last evening writing letters downstairs in the Ritz. One was to the United States; there were four to England and one to France. We have a note of the addresses. The other three people were left alone as you instructed."

Machado found coffee beans and sugar. He poured some beans into a mill and cranked the handle.

"It'll be tonight. I haven't told Szily yet."

Cabral's eyes came alive. "How do you know?"

Machado added a pinch of salt and waited till the water was boiling. He threw the ground coffee into the kettle and added a wood shaving. "Hamilton called a travel agency and asked for a reservation for tomorrow."

"And Penha Longa?"

Machado lifted the kettle from the gas and unhooked two mugs from the dresser.

"Like a beleaguered castle. The drawbridge is up and there are archers on the ramparts. I have a feeling that I shall be asked to inspect them when I get back."

Cabral shook his head. "You mean you're actually allowing Szily to go through with this crazy plan?"

Machado filled the two mugs and placed one on the table in front of Cabral. "You'd better get this very clear in your mind, Luis. It isn't me. It's His Excellency the Minister of Justice. Szily had him on the phone at nine o'clock this morning."

Cabral spoke with swift certainty. "Then one's as insane as the other."

"I've decided that Szily isn't insane." Machado wagged his finger at his side. "He sees himself as a kind of medieval priest defending a holy place against sacrilege. What's more, I have a feeling that he will do it in style."

Cabral swirled the liquid in his mug, staring down at it. "Have you been inside the museum yet?"

"No," said Machado. "I haven't asked nor has he offered."

Cabral looked up. "Doesn't it strike you that there's something very strange about all this?"

"Yes," said Machado. "But then I'm only concerned with one thing, the capture of Kosky. And what could be stranger than that? No, if Szily wants his moment of glory, let him have it."

The cat was weaving and wreathing in front of Cabral. He watched it moodily.

"You're not worried about the Scavengers?"

Machado wagged his head. "I was, but no more. I'd give a month's pay to see their faces when I make my report. The illustrious Inspectors of Cause peering up each other's asses in search of treason to the state. What time do you intend having the men here?"

"Six," said Cabral. "There's no sense in pulling them out here before. There'll be two radio cars, two teams, someone by the phone at all times."

Machado nodded, satisfied. "I'm going to hold Kosky at headquarters. I'm not letting him out of my hands."

"And the others?"

Macho shrugged indifferently. "We'll think about it. One thing at a time. I'll be at home until four if you need me."

It was half-an-hour later than that when he left the bungalow in Mem Martins. He dropped his wife at the nursery where she sometimes helped, waiting till she turned to wave goodbye, surrounded by chattering children. He turned the Renault west and drove out to Penha Longa. The ornate gates were shut. He touched the horn-ring. The keeper let him in. The man had left his shotgun in the lodge as instructed. Water was slapping the sides of the pool as if someone had just been using it. The drawing-room door was open, the curtains billowing in the breeze, but there was no sign of Szily. Machado drove around the front of the house and into the stableyard. A dark blue Mercedes limousine stood next to an Opel station wagon in the garage. There were six box stalls. A kennel with a runway completed the square. A couple of black-and-tan Dobermans clawed at the heavy-gauge wire, snarling as Machado went by. He leaned over the half-door of the end box stall. The man inside was ankle deep in clean straw, grooming the iron-gray stallion with a wisp of hay. His tanned back and shoulders glistened with sweat. He was in his late twenties with the blond hair and green eyes of someone from the Minho. His shirt was hanging on the manger together with a faded paratrooper's cap.

"Frederico?" asked Machado.

The groom suspended his strapping. "*Si, si,* Senhor. Frederico Coelho." His accent matched his coloring.

"Do you know who I am?"

"*Si,* Senhor Inspector."

"I told that idiot at the gate to put the shotgun away. We don't want the place to appear in a state of siege."

"No, Senhor." There was no offense taken, no explanation, nothing more than a smile.

Machado reached down to pull back the bolt. The stallion's ears flattened immediately. The groom grabbed the animal's tail and hissed soothingly.

"No further, Senhor," he warned. "He doesn't like strangers."

Machado pulled back hastily. "You served in Africa, I understand?"

"Two years in Moçambique. The Inspector has been there?" He bent down, feeling the stallion's tendons.

"Never," said Machado. "Things were different in my day. We had colonies and there were no problems. I did my military service thirty kilometers from my home."

The groom's smiled flashed. He nudged the gray over with his shoulder. "The Senhor Inspector rides?"

"A burro," Machado replied. "From what I see here, this animal lives better than many human beings." He glanced at the silky oats, the tarred net of sweet hay, the water trough that was replenished automatically.

"Possibly." The groom seemed to pay the idea small attention.

"Tell me," said Machado. "This is a good place to work?"

This time there was a positive reaction. Frederico's green eyes were very steady.

"This is my home, Senhor." It was plain that as far as he was concerned the dialogue had ended.

Machado returned to his room and rang the veterinarian's number. The voice that answered was glum.

"Cabral."

"Just checking," said Machado. "I was thinking about Kohn, Luis. Better take your tail off. He'll probably be seeing the others and it's no time to alarm them."

"I already did it," Cabral said shortly. "When does your friend get back?"

"Saramento? Don't worry about it. Eat whatever you can find if you're hungry. He knows what's going on."

"There's one thing he doesn't know," Cabral said tightly. "His cat's just killed one of the neighbor's chickens. Thanks for calling."

Machado hung up and looked around the room. The bed had been made in his absence, the half-used bottle of mineral water replaced by a full one. There was a box of the cheroots that he used on the table. Express a wish and the jinn fulfilled it. The phone rang. This time it was Szily on the house line. Machado spoke first.

"All the signs are that it will be tonight."

"Excellent," said Szily. "Can you come down to the stables?"

"Now?"

"If you please." Machado put the short-barreled revolver away in a drawer and hurried out.

Six men were lined up in front of the box stalls. The horses were watching the proceedings with interest. Machado recognized Frederico and the gatekeeper; the gardener he had seen early that morning. The rest were strangers. All six wore the Szily livery of dark-green breeches and high-buttoned tunic. The Baron was standing in front of them clad in a salt-and-pepper knickerbocker suit and a Panama hat. Someone had locked the dogs away in the kennel. Szily flourished the rattan cane he was holding, addressing the row of stolid faces.

"Attention, all of you! This gentleman is a high-ranking police official."

Machado did his best to look like one. Sunshine warmed the yard, releasing the strong odor of horse manure. A lawn mower stuttered somewhere in the evening calm. Szily walked along the line, pausing now and then for effect.

"You all know what we're waiting for. The house is going to be attacked by thieves, probably tonight. There is to be no attempt to hinder these people. Your presence is a precautionary one. The guns you've been given are only for display. You will stay at your allotted posts until Frederico gives you the signal. I repeat, there's to be no shooting. Is that clear or does any of you have a question?"

Nobody answered. Szily hooked his thumbs in the belt of his jacket. "One thing more, the Inspector will tell you that the law allows a degree of force in protecting one's property."

Machado cleared his throat. "Obey your master and carry out your instructions."

He followed Szily out of the yard into the rose garden. The Bermuda grass was emerald under the spray from the water sprinklers. The Baron stopped.

"The pool's at your disposal, you know, if you'd like to use it."

Machado shook his head. The list of his shortcomings was growing longer. "I never learned to swim, Excellency."

Szily shrugged. "You said these people would try tonight. How do you know this?"

"One of them's trying to book himself out of the country. Tomorrow. May I ask a question, Senhor Baron?"

"Naturally." Szily's gaze was curious.

"Why did you want me on that charade just now?"

Szily tested the turf with his heel. "To give the men confidence. After all, you represent the forces of law and order, Inspector."

"The only law they recognize is yours," Machado said steadily.

Szily's expression was amused. He consulted his watch. "You'll have to excuse me. I have some work to do. I've sent my secretary to Lisbon for a few days. Go wherever you wish. There are some fish from Brazil that might interest you. They are carnivorous. Dinner will be served at eight." He lifted his Panama politely and walked off toward the house.

Machado circled the complex layout of paved path and high, close-clipped yew hedges and descended some steps to a sunken garden. A fountain spilled into a pool, where vividly colored fish darted under the water lily leaves. He dusted off a bench by a sundial and sat down. Life indeed had its ironies. Kosky must have pinned a lot of faith on his French passport. In a sense it was understandable. He would have assumed that if he passed the check at the airport he would be out of trouble. His visit to Portugal was strictly for apolitical reasons. Brazil was a long way away and the years had passed. The knowledge must have inspired his total confidence. The sun was sinking fast, the dancing haze of insects thinning over the water. Machado walked back leisurely to the guesthouse. At quarter-of-eight he callel Cabral. The radio cars were in position. Saramento was still on his rounds. Machado washed his hands and face. He'd changed his shirt at home and found a couple of clean handkerchiefs. He switched off the light and found that it was quite dark outside. The house was a blaze of light with the ornamental bars on the windows making patterns on the curtains. The dining room was next to the library. Szily was already there in front of the cavernous fireplace, wearing a dinner jacket and stiff wing collar. A place had been laid at each end of the long polished table. Szily touched a bellpush and invited Machado to sit down. His face was ten years younger in the gleam of the candles.

"I hope you like beef, Inspector?"

Machado bobbed his head. "I am well-trained, Excellency. I eat anything."

The meal was served by two maids. One Machado already knew, the other was a slim dark girl in her teens. He swallowed a completely clear soup that as far as he was concerned tasted of nothing. *Consommé.* The beef came rare with green beans and balls of cooked dough. Strange the way these foreigners ate. He followed the Baron's lead with the array of silver cutlery. Szily drank water with his wine, barely touching the food on his plate. From time to time he smiled thinly at Machado and raised his glass. The meal over, one of the maids cleared the table and placed a decanter and glasses in front of the Baron. He nodded at her kindly.

"Good night Maria. Don't forget that I want you all in your quarters by nine-thirty."

"*Si,* Senhor Baron." Her face was troubled with secret knowledge. "Good night, Senhor," she added, looking at Machado.

The big room was quiet in the firelight. Szily filled a glass and carried it to Machado.

"I've always wondered at the British talent for discovering the virtues of different wines. Port, Madeira and sherry, for instance. Incidentally the port from this particular cask is twenty-seven years old."

Machado held the glass to the light. "The blood of the grapes. Your health, Excellency."

Szily smiled over the rim of his uplifted glass. " 'The blood of the grapes'! An apt phrase. I like it."

The rich sweetness flowed down Machado's gullet. He wiped his lips with his napkin.

"What made you decide to employ Gunilla von Mayenfels, Excellency?"

The veined, splotched hand holding Szily's glass was without a tremor. "I was wondering when you were going to ask me that. Her father was a friend of mine."

"Was?" echoed Machado.

"Was." Szily set his glass down very carefully. "He ran his car into a tree on the night of May seven, nineteen forty-five. You see I read the file, Inspector. I read it twenty-five years ago."

"Then you knew the girl?"

Szily joined the tips of his fingers. "I paid for her schooling but I had never set eyes on her. When the time came for the catalogue to be done, I thought of Gunilla. I wanted to see her. I wanted to find out what sort of woman she had become. Let's call it a natural instinct."

The wine left a nutty aftertaste that Machado savored. "I can understand your disappointment, Senhor Baron. I read the files too. A strange business, the disappearance of that jade. I suppose Mayenfels never spoke of it?"

Szily's eyes were the color of water surrounding the tip of an iceberg. "Never. The first I heard of it was after his death. As I say, the man was my friend. It's a subject I prefer not to discuss."

"Of course," said Machado. "By the way, have you informed your insurance company?"

Szily scratched his neck. The stiff collar had left a red ring on his skin. "Do you have any idea of the value of my paintings and antiques, Inspector?"

Machado eased his belt surreptitiously. The balls of dough were lying in his stomach like lead weights.

"I am a simple man with no knowledge of these things."

Szily brushed the objection aside. "Works of art have become the objects of speculation and their value increases accordingly. There are few people left who can afford to pay the fortunes in premiums that insurance companies demand these days. The result is that most art is stored in bank vaults like bullion and no longer enjoyed. The contents of my museum are worth five million dollars and they are totally uninsured."

Machado whistled soundlessly. The news only added fresh perspective to his host's eccentricity.

Szily pushed his chair back. His napkin was kept in what looked like a ring of solid gold.

"Coffee is waiting for us in the drawing room. We'll go through."

The coffee and a decanter of brandy were on a table near the fire. Machado watched as Szily reduced the lights to a single lamp by the velvet settee. The Baron put a hood over the parrot. He had drunk almost nothing but his eyes were unnaturally bright.

"The vigil begins. You must have kept many of them before, Inspector."

"Many," Machado agreed. "Apprehension often plays tricks with a man's judgment."

The Baron extinguished the spirit lamp that had kept the coffee hot. Machado spooned sugar into his cup and lighted a cheroot.

"A Telex arrived from Scotland Yard. It seems that this Canadian has a police record in England. And we know something of one of the other men. It's probable that they'll be armed."

"Indeed?" The Baron took the news in stride.

"I thought you should know," Machado said stubbornly.

"Thank you," said Szily. "*I* shall certainly be armed and I've handled weapons all my life."

Szily stared at the fire for a moment. The olivewood burned with a clear smokeless flame. "Do you have any children, Inspector?"

Machado moved his head from side to side. After nineteen years the subject still distressed him.

"Sometimes it is best," said Szily. "Mayenfels' father was private secretary to the Kaiser. A man of courage and integrity who followed his master into exile. His son died in disgrace and his granddaughter consorts with thieves."

Machado flicked ash at the fireplace. "A man was garroted in Spain twenty-five years ago. His son is one of my best officers. There is good and bad. I try not to judge."

"I'm glad to hear it," Szily answered. An odd note of insistence crept into his voice. "I don't want this girl arrested."

Machado shrugged. "Your Excellency has a talent for producing the unexpected. Keep the girl. I have no interest in her." But his personal feeling was that a short sharp lesson would have achieved far more than some eccentric form of punishment.

"I owe it to her father's memory," Szily said primly. "There's time to spare. Do you play chess, Inspector?"

Machado smiled. "For once I can say yes."

The Baron set the board with red and white ivory pieces. The first few moves told Machado that he was outclassed but he continued to play doggedly, surrendering piece after piece rather than concede defeat.

"And mate," Szily said finally. He put the pieces back in their box. "I think you'd better leave now. I'll call the guesthouse when I need you."

"You insist on staying here alone?" Machado pitched the butt into the flames. "I could stay here with you, out of sight, wherever you liked."

Szily switched off the pedestal lamp, leaving the room lit only by firelight.

"I'm obliged for your concern, my friend, but there is really no need for it."

He gave his thin veined hand to Machado and smiled courteously.

A wind had come up outside, driving a massive black bank of cloud in to obscure the stars. Machado stood in the darkness, watching the remaining lights go out, till only two were left. One was in Szily's bedroom, the other was in the dome over the museum. He groped his way along the path back to the guesthouse.

VI

THE RINGING in Hamilton's head persisted, sawing into the half-doze he had enjoyed since light first invaded the curtains. He groped for the phone on the bedside table. Kohn came on the line.

"I'm sorry if I disturbed you."

Hamilton yawned. It was twenty of ten by his watch which meant that he had more or less slept for ten hours. Incredible.

"Do tell," he said, scratching the back of his neck.

"It's our friend," Kohn said meaningfully. "He telephoned me at eight o'clock this morning to say that he's worried about the schedule."

Hamilton rolled over on his back. Bright sunshine

lightened the curtains now and he could hear someone along the corridor running a carpet sweeper. He yawned again, this time complainingly.

"We went over all this last night. You were there. You heard him agree."

"It's only about the timing," Kohn answered soothingly. "He thinks you're cutting it too fine."

Hamilton rose on an elbow. "Look, I've been ripping things off half my life. This guy's beginning to bring me down, Philip. Tell him I don't *need* his advice."

"I already have," Kohn replied. "I just thought I'd mention it."

"You've done that," said Hamilton, "and things go exactly as we agreed. I'll meet him on Black Horse Square at half-after-ten and we drive out and pick up Gunilla. There's all the time in the world."

Kohn made a show of certainty. "Everything else is all right? There's nothing else that you need?"

"Nothing. Just keep this dude off my back and relax. You're home and dry, Philip. Take a walk or something. Try to forget the whole thing."

He hung up and swung his naked body out of bed. He'd expected the old man to get jumpy. It was inevitable. But this character Kohn had brought from Paris was supposed to know his way around. From what had been said, he'd expected some kind of Jewish Dick Tracy instead of a shifty-assed number who sucked on his back teeth. But that was the way Kohn wanted it and it was Kohn who was picking up the tabs.

He wrapped a towel around his middle and pulled the curtains back. Sunshine dappled the serried roofs. It had been touch-and-go the night before whether or not he cruised the nightclubs. The old black magic had been at work. He had money in his pocket and the city was waiting. Three years was a long time without a woman's warmth, even the kind that comes with bad champagne at a hundred bucks a throw. Seeing that South American girl in the bar downstairs had straightened him out. Not a guy in the room who hadn't envied the kid who was with her. But she just sat there, loose, cool and beautiful and in love. So be it. After that there had been no way he could have faced some hooker in a discotheque.

He opened the window wide and sucked in air till his head was dizzy. You fall out of love too but no one writes songs about it. Feelings change. As the Christian Brothers used to affirm, God's judgment was the one thing that was constant and sure. He showered and dressed before retrieving the satchel of tools from under the bed. Kohn had given him half his money in Swiss francs the night before. The big, beautifully engraved bills were as imposing as the bank that backed them. Gunilla had been on his mind. He thought of calling her but had no idea which part of the building she worked in. A woman like that in love would give what she had entirely. And her hand would still be there at the end of the road, come what may.

The lobby was full of people checking out of the hotel. He walked down past the piles of baggage on the steps and turned toward the coffee drinkers poring over their newspapers in the sidewalk cafés. Traffic was tearing up and down the wide, gently sloping Avenida. Paratroopers on leave from Guiné and Moçambique mingled with the window shoppers, their faces and necks burned dark by African heat. Each corner had its blind lottery-ticket vender, intoning the promise of fortune. The few clouds were high and white, drifting in from the Atlantic. He'd eaten the night before in a fish restaurant behind the hotel. The owner had worked the codboats off the Nova Scotian coast and promised no moon for at least another week. It was a comforting assurance.

He turned into an arcade at the bottom of the Avenida. The Global Travel Agency was tucked away at the far end. He gave his name to the honey-colored girl at a desk.

"I talked with someone yesterday about getting me on a plane to Guadeloupe. You were going to check on it for me."

"That was me," the girl smiled. "I have the information right here for you, Mr. Hamilton."

Hamilton leaned closer, following the movement of her scarlet-tipped nail as she ran through the schedule.

"There are no direct flights from Lisbon to Guadeloupe but Air France flies twice a week, Orly–Pointe-à-Pitre. That would be your best route. Tourist class is fully booked for the next month but I can get you on first class, the day after tomorrow."

He straightened up. "And from here to Paris?"

"There are two flights a day, morning and afternoon."

He turned the corners of his mouth down, thinking of landing on a plane with Kosky.

"Isn't there any other way? How about the train?"

She held her place with one hand, reaching for the schedule with the other.

"The Sur-Express. At sixteen-fifty every day. There are

sleepers and you travel overnight. It would get you to Paris in good time."

"I'm on," he said, reaching inside his pocket. "Book me! First class all the way through. I'll pay now and collect the tickets later."

He changed Swiss francs into escudos at the cashier's desk and gave her the amount she asked for. She scribbled a receipt.

"I'll have to confirm with Air France but your ticket should be ready some time after lunch. It's the first time I've ever booked anyone to Guadeloupe. Do you mind if I ask why you're going there?"

"Business," he said. No use telling her that he'd picked up an old magazine in jail. "Why?"

She smiled, her eyes far away. "My grandmother came from Guadeloupe. I hope you have a wonderful time."

"Thank you," he said. He walked the length of the arcade to the bank on the corner. He'd no idea what he was going to do under a banana tree but maybe it wasn't important anymore. The main thing was to slow down and stop running. A bank officer sold him a sterling draft for two hundred pounds payable to Albert Dean. It would take a couple of days for the letter to reach England, but the extra fifty would restore Albie's faith in human nature. The car-hire firm fifty yards away operated with the efficiency of a worldwide organization. A clerk took Hamilton's money, registered the particulars of his driving license and had him behind the wheel of a Ford Cortina in less than twelve minutes.

He drove south toward the river into a dockside area of slop-shops, hardware stores, honky-tonk bars and holes in the wall selling cheap jewelry. He parked and bought himself blue coveralls and a cap, a couple of lengths of rope and two grappling hooks, a pair of Japanese walkie-talkies in a radio store. His last call was at an uptown agency for motorcycles where he chose an Italian midget bike with small fat wheels and collapsible handlebars. A mechanic stowed it in the back of the Ford while Hamilton was paying the bill. Twenty minutes later, he was driving out of the city and heading west.

He'd eaten no breakfast and stopped at a pine-built restaurant high in the hills above Estoril. It was early and the place was empty except for a flock of peacocks stalking about stiff-legged in the garden. He ate alone at a window table: meat soup flavored with mint, pork stewed with clams and a thinly sliced orange. He washed the meal down with a bottle of good Portuguese lager and lit his first smoke of the day.

Maples and oak trees were growing in the forest on the far side of the highway. The shades of green changed as the trees dropped down toward the wide estuary. He picked out the spruce and fir he had felled on the Gaspé Peninsula. There were times when he could still hear the sound of timber crashing, the warning shouts echoing through woods as old as Canada itself. He could remember the way the mosquitoes probed delicately through sweaty clothes and skin. The beans and stewed tea, the nostalgic sound of the fat-bellied tugs as they left ahead of the floodwater. He'd learned a lot about himself during those eighteen months. To start with, he'd learned that he was no hero. Fear was something you had to accept. If you did it with a grin, the going was somehow easier. Life became a sort of book and no matter how much you had read of the story, no matter what the rest of it promised, the only pages worth reading were the ones open in front of you.

He called for his check and drank the last of his beer. Three years ago he wouldn't have touched a caper like this. A rich and slightly dotty art-dealer, a neurotic chick with a father complex and this ferret-faced freak from Paris. He'd have run from it all so fast they wouldn't have been able to time him. Yet here he was up to his neck in it. For once, instinct seemed to be stronger than judgment. The thing that still bothered him was the fact that he was working with amateurs. That's why he'd bought the motorcycle. If any of these people panicked he'd have to go on his own.

He paid the waiter and walked out to the rented car under the cypresses. He followed the route Gunilla had taken the previous day, forking left at Queluz into rocky ravines bright with yellow gorse and purple heather. His mind registered landmarks as he drove. It would be early in the morning if he had to make a run for it. The trains and buses would have stopped. He'd have to be prepared for roadblocks. The obvious places for these would be on the highway that followed the river and the autostrada to Lisbon. The map he had found in the glove compartment showed a network of secondary roads between Queluz and the capital. The small aluminum-framed bike was light enough to be carried for short distances. He could ride awhile, take to the bush, hole up if necessary. No matter how loud the alarm, they could have no idea who he was. There'd be no need for him to go back to the hotel. All he'd have to do was make the Santa Appolonia railroad station by ten minutes to five, fourteen hours maybe to cover less than eighteen miles.

The way ahead dipped sharply, snaking past red roofs, landscaped houses and ordered hedgerows joined by white-painted gates. The graded road leveled out, picking up the boundary wall of Penha Longa. The wire was still down where Gunilla had turned into the trees. He'd seen no more than a couple of cars since leaving Queluz and those had been going in the opposite direction. He averted his face as he passed the closed entrance to Szily's estate. The boundary wall continued to run parallel to the road for another half-mile before turning sharply north. He pulled onto the rutted track that followed the line of the wall and stopped after a couple of hundred yards. It was very quiet here between the wall and the thicket of poplars. Bees droned in the gorse and butterflies tasted the wildflowers. It was like a June day. He sat on a rock and lit a cigarette. The end of Szily's driving range was behind the stone wall at his back. There was only one exit from Penha Longa. If it came to the worst, the hunt would center on the house and the gate lodge. But, even at night, a man who knew precisely where he was going could cover the stretch of Bermuda grass at the dead run, scale the wall and be away.

He finished his smoke slowly, walked back to the car and unlocked the trunk. A cogged wheel unlocked the handlebars of the small machine. He straddled the bike and kicked down on the starter. The motor caught instantly, purring away with the smoothness of a sewing machine. He silenced it, stuffed the coveralls and cap under the saddle and wheeled the bike into the bushes. He taped the map to the gas tank and laid the machine on its side. When he looked back from the track there was nothing to see. The next thing was to tie a length of rope to one of the grapnels and heave the weight at the top of the wall. The hook caught and he went up hand-over-hand and peered over. The bridle path was immediately beneath him, bordered by lavender and rosemary. He hung on with one hand, coiled the rope on the hook and slung it into the bushes. It sank there without trace. He fixed the spot in his mind by the red flag on the driving green, dropped down again and walked back to the car.

A startled jay planed away out of the poplars, its call grating and strident. Penha Longa was marked on the map they had given him.

There were various ways back to Lisbon. One thing was certain. The motorbike would go wherever the car went. He turned the ignition key. After five hundred yards the track veered into the trees. He shifted into low gear, climbing up through hummocks of earth riddled with rabbit holes, then down again to ford a moss-banked stream. The track ran out of the poplars across a rocky field and stopped at a padlocked gate. Beyond the gate was a potholed lane. He used the tire iron on the padlock and edged the Ford through. He closed the gate and rehung the padlock. The sun gave him a sense of direction. The first sign he came to read CASCAIS 12 KM.

It was just after five when he put the car away in the underground garage at the bottom of the Avenida da Liberdade. He collected the tickets from the travel agency and walked up to the hotel. The receptionist appeared to remember him. There were no calls, no messages. He crossed the thronged lobby, swinging his shoulders unconsciously like a fighter coming out for the last round. Upstairs, he lay on the bed, studying the flight ticket. The magazine article had spoken of an island in the Leeward group, people of African stock with Creole, East Indian and European minorities. He had a quick flash of himself in years to come, in some bar on a tropical beach, fat and unshaven, wearing a dirty white suit and looking like the late Sydney Greenstreet. The barman would be on the order of Humphrey Bogart and he'd have heard all Hamilton's stories too many times. They'd be standing there in silence, the two of them, listening to the tattoo of rain beating down on a tin roof while dead dogs washed in on the surf. He shook his head, breaking the nightmare vision. Guadeloupe, Dominica, Grenada, Trinidad. With money in his pocket he could hop from one island to another.

It was seven when the phone rang. He picked it up. The Lisbon air seemed to have benefited Kohn's breathing.

"Scott?"

Hamilton leaned back against the headboard. "What's on your mind, Philip?"

Kohn sounded both hurt and surprised. "Well, for one thing this could be our last talk together!"

"That's life," said Hamilton. "I intended to call you in any case. You still owe me some money."

"Gunilla has it. You've made your travel arrangements?"

This was the prison visitor asking if the food was edible, concerned but not too deeply.

"All ready to go," said Hamilton.

"Is there any chance that you'll be coming back to England?"

Hamilton stared through the window. Black clouds were assembling in the west. The daffodils and crocuses would be out in the London parks and the cops would be after his ass.

"I doubt it but every time I say something like that I wind up with egg on my face."

Kohn's voice was regretful. "Well, you know where I live."

"That's right."

Kohn cleared his throat. "You won't forget that Kosky makes the delivery?"

"I won't forget," answered Hamilton. It was Kohn's own brand of insurance and from his point of view it made sense. Jews took care of their own.

"It leaves everyone free to make his own way out," Kohn said easily.

"I'm all in favor of it." Hamilton sat up straight. "When are you off?"

"On the afternoon flight. I'm going by way of Berlin. I have a friend there who's taking care of the paperwork. There'll be documents that I need, naturally. I suppose this is really goodbye, Scott."

"I guess so," said Hamilton. There was no suggestion that anything might go wrong, an assumption of infallibility that was heady stuff. "Everything I said before — you know, I'm grateful, Philip. It's been a good one. Look after yourself."

"You too, Scott."

Hamilton hung up with a feeling that something had

been left unsaid but he couldn't determine what. He changed his shirt and checked the contents of his pockets. Passport, tickets and money. The tools and bottle of aniseed were in the trunk of the car with the other things. He took his coat with him, gloves and the room key. With any luck he'd sleep in the hotel, if not he was at least mobile. He rode the elevator down to the lobby. The receptionist glanced across from his place at the desk. Hamilton smiled. The guy looked as if he had problems.

The garage had emptied, leaving the Ford sticking out like a single black note on a piano keyboard. He headed it up the ramp, staying with the southbound rush of traffic till he made a left on Rossio. Five minutes later he was jolting over the cobbles outside the Santa Apollonia railroad station. He locked his car and made his way into the noise and confusion inside. The list of daily departures was up on the big board. Track 10 SUR EXPRESS 16.50 RESTAURANTE E WAGONS-LITS. The first stop was Salamanca in Spain. Lisbon was the only place the train could be boarded in Portugal. He memorized the layout of the station, Track 10 in relation to the exits. The barriers opened half an hour before departure time. The doubt that had been riding him had gone completely. With any kind of luck he'd be back in the hotel long before Szily discovered his loss. After that he'd be just another tourist among thousands of others in Lisbon. All he was doing was hedging his bet. He'd done it in the old days and the investment had always proved a wise one.

VII

HE ATE in a nearby restaurant, killing time over endless cups of coffee till his watch showed quarter-after-ten. He drank no liquor, sticking to a rule he had made years before. There'd be plenty of time to drink afterward. He'd seen a lot of good guys walk themselves into the slammer, freaked out on booze. He turned the car around and drove west, stopping on a vast square that was open on the south side to the river. The whole city rose in lights to the north. Lamplit colonnaded buildings surrounded the square on three sides. He wheeled the Ford in close to the giant statue, killed the motor and stuck a cigarette in his mouth. Traffic was dense all around but the center of the square was an oasis with no more than a handful of parked cars. Taxis were unloading outside the ferry station. The lights of the Salazar Bridge showed against the night, eighty tons of steel suspended from the city to the Setubal peninsula and beneath it the dark deep river.

A movement caught his eye and he turned his head quickly. Kosky came creeping around the base of the statue, like a mongoose hunting a snake, swinging from side to side, his hands deep in his pockets. He was wearing the same boxy tweed suit and shoes with one-inch rubber heels. Hamilton opened the passenger door, leaned out and whistled softly.

Kosky climbed in beside Hamilton, shifted the gum he was chewing and nodded. "Shalom!"

"Are you feeling all right?" Hamilton asked curiously.

Kosky's eyes glittered. "I'm not the worrying kind."

Hamilton backed the rented car out and drove west along the waterfront. On the left were the docks and the tall blank walls of warehouses. There was a strong smell of tar and seaweed. The traffic signal ahead blinked red. A small locomotive came into view hauling a line of flat-cars across the narrow-gauge tracks. Rusted and barnacled ships were discharging freight under the glare of arc lamps. A tug wallowed out toward the mouth of the estuary, a nostalgic blast on its foghorn lingering behind.

Kosky's jaws moved steadily. He watched the train till it disappeared at the side of the Maritime Police Station.

Hamilton glanced sideways. "Kohn said you were worried about the schedule."

Kosky bared his teeth in a token smile, still chewing, but he made no answer.

The motor raced under the probe of Hamilton's toe.

"You know, you bug me," he said suddenly. "There's something about you that doesn't add up."

Kosky suspended his chewing momentarily. "You mean I don't act the way you think I should? It is something to do with my manner?"

"You could say that, yes. In fact, yes to both questions," answered Hamilton.

The changing signal imparted a greenish hue to Kosky's face. "You talk too much and you smile too much. I need neither of these things."

They eyed one another for a second, Hamilton drumming his fingers on the steering wheel. Short of a swift poke in the nose, he could think of no adequate way of dealing with the insult. He let the clutch in with a jerk and they drove on in silence. The traffic was heavier now. They passed a succession of empty beaches smelling of mud, walled summer homes and high-rise apartment buildings of unparalleled ugliness. Hamilton turned north at Estoril into the hills. Praia de Pera was asleep, the market square deserted except for a solitary cop smoking under a sign advertising sewing machines. Cats streaked in the shadows as they drove up the alley. Hamilton took a right, cut the motor and coasted down the narrow street past shuttered and curtained houses. A newspaper lifted on the wind and soared over the roofs like a gull. He stopped the car at the end of the street, where a crumbling parapet guarded the edge of the cliff.

"I'll go get her."

Kosky offered the guarded nod of someone who meets a stranger on a lonely stretch of road. It was the first time either man had spoken since leaving Lisbon. The door opened as Hamilton reached for the bellpush. He slipped inside the house quickly. The living-room fire was almost out and the ashtray littered with butts.

He looked at Gunilla. Her hair was tied in a scarf. She was wearing dark bell-bottom trousers, a blazer and rope-soled beach shoes. He smiled encouragingly.

"Are you scared?"

Her blue stare was steady. "Yes, but not too much."

"Nothing's going to happen to you, honey," he said. "Get that into your head. *Nothing!*"

The freckles across her nose seemed to be splashed on with paint. "I won't let you down."

He touched her cheek with the palm of his hand. "I know it." He unfastened the french windows and went down the steps. The carton in the shed was exactly as he had left it. He untied the string. The hare crouched among its droppings, nose twitching. He put the cover back on the box and carried it into the house.

"Let's go!"

He opened the door and looked right and left cautiously. The lamps hanging from the walls creaked in the wind, shafts of light falling across the façades of the silent houses.

Gunilla lengthened her stride to match his, keeping very close to him, her fingertips just touching his elbow. Kosky's head reared up as they neared the car.

"She drives," said Hamilton. "You go in back."

He took the passenger seat, watching Gunilla make a dry run through the gears and testing the headlights. Her voice was uncertain.

"There are two ways from here to Penha Longa. They're both about the same distance. If you have a map I can show you."

She was wearing the scent Hamilton remembered and looked strangely boyish and vulnerable in her blazer and bell-bottomed trousers. He put the carton on the floor and placed his foot on it. The animal inside had started to kick violently.

"Take the way you know best, and, easy, there's plenty of time."

She drove out past a cemetery, making a detour around the sleeping village. The road unwound in the staring headlights; the trees ahead seemed to lean in and form a tunnel. Gunilla handled the car confidently, carving her way through the darkness. Her face was withdrawn and preoccupied. They passed no other traffic for twenty kilometers. She shifted down to second as they started the long twisting descent.

"We're almost there — another kilometer."

She cut her headlights to minimum. The gates leading to Szily's estate were shut tight, the lodge still and silent. Hamilton leaned forward, looking for the gap in the wire. He saw it and pointed.

"Straight in, slowly."

She turned the car through the sagging fenceposts. Dirt spattered the sides of the car as it crawled forward and made a U-turn. She cut her lights and the motor and wiped her mouth with the back of her hand. Hamilton could feel the tremor in her body. The wind was making the tops of the trees sway but the floor of the forest was warm and quiet. He took a deep breath and faced them both.

"OK. This is it."

Kosky's gum clicked. He was stuffing the bottoms of his trousers into his socks. The maneuver irritated Hamilton for some reason.

"Let's get one thing straight," he said. "From here on in, I'm the man who gives the orders."

Gunilla nodded. Kosky's face was bored. "Do what I tell you," promised Hamilton, "and this thing's going to be simple. I don't give a goddamn whether or not you agree with me, as long as you do what I say."

He eased his collar. He was starting to sweat and his mouth was dry.

"You've said all this before," remarked Kosky. "Why don't we just get on with it."

Gunilla's eyes were watchful in the light of her cigarette. She was looking at Hamilton as if it were important for her to remember his face. He unlocked the trunk and came back with both arms loaded. He dropped one of the walkie-talkies in Gunilla's lap and pressed a button on the other. She jumped as a buzzer sounded.

"That's the call signal," he explained. "Keep away from yours. I don't want to be walking around in the house with that kind of noise!"

She concentrated, following the movements of his fingers as he explained the simple controls.

"On. Off. Call. The odds are against us having to use these things but if we do, I want you to move fast. Don't argue or panic. Just do whatever I say. You won't be left behind, don't worry about it."

She managed an uncertain smile. Kosky's voice cut in. "Are we going to sit here all night or what?"

Hamilton strapped on the second walkie-talkie so that it was flat against his chest. The tools, penlight and the bottle of aniseed were in the pockets of his leather coat, his passport, money and tickets buttoned on his hip. He was sweating profusely now, his nerve-ends taut with expectation. He checked the knot fastening the half-inch hemp to the grapnel hook. Gunilla was still watching him intently, Kosky sitting quiet and mean in the back. Hamilton winked at Gunilla, picked up the rope and hook and turned to the Brazilian.

"Keep your voice down once we're over that wall. Talk with your hands."

Kosky opened his door. Both men trotted toward the empty stretch of road, their rubber-soled shoes making no sound as they crossed the hardtop.

Hamilton glanced back once but the car was completely hidden in the dark forest. He threw the hook up. It caught, first time. He could hear the wind whistling in the trees on the other side of the wall. He squatted down, opened the carton and grabbed the buck by its ears. It hung quietly enough till he emptied the bottle of aniseed into its fur. Then it started to struggle violently. Kosky helped him up the rope; Hamilton supported himself on the top of the wall with his elbows and let the animal fall. It jackknifed up, spraying sand as it huddled along the bridle path. Kosky's face was a blob of white below. All Hamilton could hear was the moan of the wind. He slid down the rope.

"There's something funny going on — I don't hear the dogs."

The Brazilian's eyes were suspicious. "Why not, what's wrong?" he whispered.

Hamilton moved a hand doubtfully. "It must be the wind. They're probably half a mile away by now. Up you go!"

Kosky showed no sign of moving. Hamilton touched him on the shoulder encouragingly.

"Come on, let's go."

Kosky shook himself free. "You go first."

Hamilton brought his face close to Kosky's, snarling. "Get up that goddamn rope, you bastard. I'll lay you out cold if I have to!"

The Brazilian went into a half-crouch, watching Hamilton, his face venomous.

Suddenly he turned and went up the rope like a monkey. He straddled the top, leaned down and gave Hamilton a hand. The grapnel was reversed so that the rope now hung on the inside of the wall.

The two men dropped to the bridle path and ran forward into the gum trees. The ropes of leaves swayed in the wind like wraiths, clinging to their shoulders as they pushed on deeper. Suddenly Hamilton stopped and chopped his arm down, signaling for absolute silence. A high-pitched howling came through the night. Memory identified the sound as the complaint of a frustrated animal. The dogs had been confined somewhere and sensed that strangers were abroad.

He waved Kosky on, ignoring the question in the other man's eyes. The house ahead offered a silent façade that was seemingly impregnable. They trotted lightly over the gravel to the side door and stood for a while with their backs flat against the wall. Hamilton shifted his head cautiously. The dogs had stopped their howling. He glanced through the nearest window. Firelight flickered beyond the curtains. A clock chimed somewhere inside. He unfastened the satchel of tools and felt among the contents with gloved fingers. His eyes and ears seemed to be on stalks, probing the air for danger like antennae.

He switched on the penlight and let the tiny beam travel down the door. The key had been left in the lock on the other side, the tip just showing in the keyhole. He climbed the forceps on the end of the shank and turned his wrist anticlockwise. He felt the tumblers lift and engage. He spanned the door, marking the position of the top bolt. The battery-driven drill ate into the wood, boring a hole an eighth of an inch in diameter. He fed a loop of piano wire through the hole, easing it gently along till the loop caught the head of the bolt. A quick jerk released it. He did the same thing with the lower bolt and pushed. The door swung backward silently.

The inner door was open. He beckoned Kosky into the quiet warmth of the drawing room and stood stock-still, listening to the sounds behind the silence. Wind echoed down the chimney. A joist settled in the roof. Kosky's head was swinging from side to side, his jaws moving incessantly. Hamilton lifted the coffeepot and held it against his cheek. It was stone cold. There were two dirty cups on the silver tray, a brandy decanter and one unused glass. A dead, half-smoked cheroot lay in the ashtray. That would be the man he had seen in the pool, the secretary. The last of the fire burned with a clear hungry blaze that briefly lit the corners of the vast shadowy room. The parrot was by the window with a hood over its cage. He tapped his pockets to make sure that nothing jingled and turned the handle of the door leading to the corridor. The firelight behind him illuminated the line of plaster saints. They inched forward as far as the library. Hamilton shone the tiny flashbeam on the folds of tapestry. The heavy steel door was closed, as he had known it must be.

He signaled Kosky to stay where he was and tiptoed along to the hallway. Glass eyes in the stuffed heads on the wall reflected the light from his flash. The wide staircase on his left was covered with deep blue carpet held by angled brass rods. He moved toward it, sweat dropping on his ribs, but with certainty of remembered skills. He felt his way up the handrail, keeping his weight well to one side. The staircase ended on a landing that was overlaid with the same blue carpet. A large bowl of roses stood on a marquetry chest under a window. He could see the shapes of the swaying trees beyond the panes of glass. There was only one door and it was open.

He cocked his head at the darkness beyond. Gradually he detected the sound of rhythmic snoring. He kept the penlight switched on but held it between his teeth, leaving his hands free. Then he stepped forward warily, directing the beam toward the foot of the bedside table. Szily was lying flat on his back, his head deep in the pillows. He was wearing gray silk pajamas. His teeth were out, his arms folded on his chest, and he was snoring. His pulsing throat made a soft growling sound at the end of each exhalation. There was an empty water tumbler on the table, a small bottle next to it. Hamilton read the label. NOLUDAR 300. Sleeping pills. Everything Gunilla had said about the house and Szily to date had turned out to be accurate so the key had to be somewhere in this room. Under the pillow, Gunilla had said.

He switched his gaze from the bedside table back to Szily's face. The Baron's nostrils were flared, his open mouth exposing the bare gums. Adrenalin pumped into Hamilton's bloodstream. Once before, it seemed a lifetime ago, he had lifted a sleeping head, intent on the jewels beneath the pillow. The woman had waked, her eyes staring up into his without perception, her brain still locked in a dream. He had put her down with infinite care, fear freezing his arms, his heart banging as her eyes closed again. He'd crouched by the side of the bed, listening to the sound of her breathing. He could see the diamond bracelet and had taken it with the delicacy of a settling mosquito.

He reached beneath Szily's pillow. No key. For the first time Gunilla's information was inaccurate.

The flashlight was getting warm in his mouth. He swallowed the gathering spittle. Szily was no parvenu. The key would be somewhere more obvious. There was nothing on the top of the dressing table but a set of ivory-backed brushes. His reflection stared back at him from the tiled mirror like the ghost of a drowning man, hair hanging over its forehead. He eased the right-hand drawer open and felt among the neatly folded socks. Nothing. The left-hand drawer offered only handkerchiefs. He raised his head. The beam from the flash shone on a small leather purse hanging from the swivel of the oval mirror. He touched it hopefully, feeling the hardness of metal inside and opened the purse. The slim key was notched on both sides and carried the maker's name on the shaft: ROSSITER SECURITY SYSTEMS.

He took the penlight out of his mouth, thumbed it off and backed out of the room. He stood on the landing, holding his breath till the sawing sound of Szily's breathing reassured him. He went down the stairs very quickly. Kosky was waiting for him in the library doorway. The Brazilian's lips curled back as Hamilton held up the key. Hamilton's gesture warned of the need for caution. He lifted the folds of the tapestry, feeling along the smooth steel surface till he found the lock. He pushed the key in and turned it twice, once to the left and once to the right. A motor whirred and the massive door started to slide back into the wall. The tapestry muffled the sound but to Hamilton's ears the noise was deafening.

The light from the glass dome ahead was no more than a paler shade of darkness. The shapes in the museum were vague and without substance. Gunilla's sketches and description had given him a fair idea of the way the place had been constructed. It was a shell within an outer shell. From the outside the windows on the north and east of the house were the same as the rest. But the doors and corridors to be seen through them were fake and led nowhere.

His ears detected the faint hum of the air-conditioning unit that maintained the temperature constant through winter and summer. He switched the flash on again. The shaft of light journeyed along the walls. Icons and paintings were hung in clusters, the names of the artists inscribed on small oval plates. Some of the names were familiar. Corot, Monet, Watteau, Ruysdael. There were landscapes, tranquil scenes of village life, portraits of satin-clothed aristocrats dancing, the somber fields of battle. Between the groups of paintings a profusion of jewels and antiques were displayed in handsome cases. Delicately tinted porcelain, jeweled dagger-scabbards, an Egyptian death mask in beaten gold, a rope of black pearls, a carved alabaster hand holding an uncut emerald. An Aramaic testament blazed on a Gothic priedieu. Each article had been chosen both for its antiquity and its beauty. The display cases were locked.

A straight-backed chair in the middle of the carpet faced a gilt mirror on the wall. Beside it on the floor was an empty glass. The sweat gathered cold in Hamilton's armpits. His shirt was sticking to his back. He made the tour of the fifty-foot-long room, shining his light into the display vases. Kosky used matches on the other side of the room. The two men met at the entrance and Hamilton shook his head. He checked his watch. Twenty after one. The jade was somewhere here, it had to be.

He turned slowly, looking at the chair in the middle of the carpet. The mirror on the wall drew him like a magnet. He crossed the room and lifted the mirror off the hook. Behind it was a small safe set chest-high in the wall. As he spun the combination dial tentatively, the museum flooded with light. Baron Szily was standing behind them both, wearing a cashmere robe over his pajamas. His teeth were in and his pale blue eyes were threatening. He poked at them, with the heavy Luger he was holding.

"Stand back to back with your hands in the air."

There was nothing old or indecisive in the way he spoke and carried himself. A concealed door was open in the paneling. Hamilton saw the flight of stairs that led up to Szily's bedroom. His arms were high above his head and he felt Kosky's shoulders wedged against his own. The Brazilian's body was stiff with tension. Szily circled them and came close to Hamilton, his hooked nose questing.

"Who sent you here? Why have you come to rob me?"

Hamilton stared into the end of the gun, seeing the prison cell beyond it. The years stretched into eternity. There was no answer left to give, nothing to say. The walkie-talkie strapped to his chest was useless and there was no way of warning the girl. Szily's eyes were bright, the pulse-beat fast in his shriveled neck. He stepped back a pace and brought the automatic near to Kosky's head.

"You then, who sent you here?"

Kosky answered in rapid Portuguese. Hamilton heard him as if in a dream. The gun swung back at Hamilton.

"Is that true? You admit it? Gunilla Mayenfels sent you here?"

Hamilton shook his head. "I don't know what you're talking about."

Baron Szily's face set hard. "Then I shall help you remember. You are vandals, going armed by night. This house is surrounded by my men. I can still let you go free, only first I want the truth."

Hamilton's tongue sneaked out and wet his lips. Suddenly it all fell into place. The dogs confined in their kennel, the charade with sleeping pills, the key hanging where he must find it. He shook his head again.

"You're wasting your . . . "

He bit the sentence in half, stumbling forward under the sudden backward thrust of Kosky's shoulders. He felt his scalp split as the Baron chopped down with the gun, then the blood ran warm in his hair. He looked up from his knees. The Luger was on the floor ten feet away. Kosky had the Baron's head wrenched back in a savage hold. The Brazilian's free hand was holding a gun with a silencer, the muzzle jammed tight against the old man's temple.

"Que é o segrêdo do cofre?" he demanded, pointing at the safe.

The pulse in Szily's neck jumped erratically. Hamilton climbed to his feet warily, stanching the flow of blood with his handkerchief. Kosky picked up the Luger, ejected the magazine and dropped the shells in his pocket.

"O segrêdo!" he insisted.

Szily's face had gone the color of a mushroom. He was trying to speak but his mouth worked despairingly. Kosky ripped his gun through the nearest painting. He spoke to Hamilton in English.

"Get over by the safe. This old bastard is going to give you the combination."

Baron Szily's eyes pleaded with them both. "There is a police inspector in the guesthouse. He'll do whatever I say. I'll give you money."

The Brazilian's expression was implacable. He used his gunsight like a chisel on a Flemish triptych. Flakes of paint showed on the carpet. Szily wrenched the words out with an effort.

"Two-three-seven-nine-left. Five-five-two-zero-right."

"Open it!" ordered Kosky.

Hamilton spun the dial. His scalp wound was shallow. His hair was matted but the bleeding had stopped. He locked the last digit in place and pulled the handle. The safe door swung open. There was a flat leather box on the lower shelf, an envelope on top of it. He lifted the box out and pressed the catch. Jeweled eyes winked at him from a bed of black velvet. Never in his life had he seen anything quite as beautiful. He held the case out to Kosky. As the Brazilian pored over the five jade dragons, Hamilton slipped the envelope into his pocket. Kosky's gun had come as a surprise. He closed the safe and spun the dial. A deep gasp made him turn his head. The Baron staggered back against the wall, clutching at his chest, eyes wide in an ashen face. His legs buckled suddenly and he seemed to collapse in sections. His shoulders scraped down the wall and his head thudded on the carpet. He kicked once spasmodically and lay still. The two men moved forward at the same time. Hamilton was first to reach the prostrate body. He knelt by its side and lifted a limp wrist. There was no pulse, no indication of breathing. The pale blue eyes glazed as he stared into them. He wiped his hands carefully on the front of his jacket and climbed up, wanting to vomit.

"He's dead," he said flatly.

Kosky came closer. He poked the muzzle of his gun against Szily's cheek and twisted it. The only result was a bruising mark on the livid cheek. The glazed eyes were completely unconscious of the viciousness.

Hamilton pulled himself upright. The man was dead and he needed reassurance.

"You saw what happened," he said defensively. "It must have been his heart."

The gun lifted in Kosky's hand, aiming straight at Hamilton's stomach. "And what happens now, Mr. Professional?" the Brazilian asked softly.

Hamilton backed off. "I know what happens to me. I'm getting out of here fast. It's our only chance. Separate and make a run for it."

Kosky came after him, talking now with a ferocity of purpose. "Run *where?* Do you think he was bluffing! This place is surrounded. What kind of a fool are you?"

Hamilton shook his head. The gash on his scalp felt as if it had been hemstitched with steel wire. Anything was better than just staying here and waiting to be captured.

"You've got what we came for," he said cautiously, nodding at the box under Kosky's arm. "Do what you like. Me, I'm going to warn the girl and get the hell out of it."

He was unstrapping the walkie-talkie when Kosky fired. There was only a short distance between them and Hamilton felt the heat of the flash. Gas leaked from the vents in the silencer. The *splat* of the explosion dwindled in the confined space. Hamilton turned his head involuntarily. The .38-caliber shell had plowed through a display case and embedded itself in the paneling.

Kosky's dark eyes were intense "*I* give the orders now! We're leaving with this as hostage." He touched Szily's body with the tip of his shoe.

"You're out of your mind," Hamilton said, staring back with disbelief.

"For everyone else he's alive." Kosky shifted his jaw.

The gum was still in his mouth. "I know exactly what I'm doing."

Hamilton swallowed furtively, glancing at the slashed paintings on the wall. The stink of exploded cordite still pervaded the room. This guy would stop at nothing.

"And me?"

Kosky dropped the gun back in his pocket. His left arm was clamping the box of jade tight to his side. "If you want to stay alive, you come with me, and you do as you're told."

There was a hard edge to the words, an implicit threat that whatever Hamilton's choice, Kosky would be able to handle it.

Hamilton searched the Brazilian's face. "What are you going to do about Gunilla?"

"We need her," said Kosky. "Worry about yourself, my friend." Hamilton fingered his blood-matted hair. The man was completely cool and his confidence inspired a perverse sort of hope.

"OK," he said. "Let's get out!"

Kosky hung on the words for a second and then nodded. "Secure the doors at the back of the house. Make sure that no one can come in from outside."

Hamilton ran back to the drawing room, double-locked the doors and removed the keys. He rammed the bolts home. Nobody else was likely to be carrying piano wire. The fire was no more than a heap of red and gray ash. There was no light to betray him from outside as he tested the bars on the windows. He could hear Kosky at the front of the house. He ran back along the corridor, overturning a plaster saint in his haste to reach the museum.

Kosky was standing by the Baron's body. He'd put the jade down somewhere. His arms were free. A bulge in his pocket showed that he had kept the gun. He bent over Szily.

"Give me a hand to get him up to the bedroom."

They dragged the body through the door in the paneling and up the short flight of stairs. The secret passage ended in a clothes-closet in the bedroom. The closet doors were open. They pushed through rows of hanging suits and lifted the body on top of the bed.

"Get your head cleaned up," ordered Kosky. "I'll put some clothes on him."

The bathroom was fitted with a black marble tub and silver faucets. Greenery was growing in a porcelain tub. A medicine chest stood beside the full-length mirror. Hamilton found scissors inside, iodoform and a roll of adhesive tape. He closed the gash with a strip of tape and toweled his face, neck and hair dry. As he bent to drop the bloodied towel in the laundry basket, lights came on outside. The dogs were howling again. He hurried back into the bedroom. Szily's body was already dressed in charcoal-gray flannel trousers and brown shoes. Kosky was zipping a waterproof golf jacket over the pajama top. Szily's eyes were still wide, his lips dark-purple in a mask of yellowed skin.

Hamilton leaned against the bedpost. "A light's just come on outside. I think it's in the guesthouse."

Kosky pulled the top half of Szily's body erect and threaded himself under a shoulder.

"Get the other arm. We'll take him down to the library."

They carried their burden downstairs slowly, the dead man's legs trailing. They propped him up in a library chair. Kosky's trousers had burst out of his socks. The box with the jade in it was on the table in front of him. He sat down and lifted the house phone. He spoke in Portuguese, his tone full of authority. Hamilton's ears strained, chasing each word without understanding. Kosky put the receiver down.

"The police inspector. He wants to speak to Szily."

Hamilton blocked his growing nausea. "You can't fake it. Nor can I."

"There is no need," Kosky said, leaning back in his chair. "I've given him two minutes to make up his mind. If they don't accede to our terms, Szily dies."

There was a macabre air of reality in what he said that made Hamilton glance instinctively at the inert body. The seconds ticked away. He imagined the ring of lights as he bolted for the trees, the unleashed dogs baying as they closed in on him. The phone came to life, jarring the silence.

Kosky spoke briefly and was on his feet in a flash.

"They've accepted. Tell the girl to bring the car to the front of the house. Tell her to wait with the motor running until we come out. They're opening the front gates for her now."

Hamilton wrestled the walkie-talkie free and hoisted the antenna. Please God she was still there. He thumbed the call-button, holding the set close to his ear. It crackled, then Gunilla's voice came on the air. He cut her off and spoke urgently.

"No questions, just get to the house as fast as you can. Come to the front door and keep the motor running!"

He collapsed the antenna and slung the set over his shoulder. Doubt and remorse flared. It *had* to be some kind of trap. He should have told her to run for it instead of bringing her into the trap. They'd be no more than one jump ahead of the police. Whatever happened to her now, he'd have done it.

"Lift him!" ordered Kosky.

Hamilton took his share of the dead man's weight and they carried him through to the hall. A match flared in Kosky's fingers, illuminating the grinning masks on the wall. They wedged Szily in a corner of the oak settle. The muscles of his neck no longer supported his head. It lolled forward helplessly.

Hamilton's voice was aghast. "We're never going to get away with it, for crissakes! They're going to *see* that he's dead."

Kosky's answer was low and savage. "Pull yourself together! I told them he'd had a heart attack and needs a doctor."

The two men stationed themselves at the windows, one on each side of the front door. The lights outside had been extinguished. The guesthouse and servants' quarters were no more than silhouettes against the dark sky. Hamilton's hand was deep in his pocket, hanging on to the envelope he had taken from the safe as if it were a talisman. Instinct told him to hide it from Kosky. He delved deeper and found his cigarettes. His fingers were perfectly steady. His brain seemed to have achieved a strange objectivity.

There was no going back on the route he had chosen but he could still keep faith with the people who trusted him. If he only had that at the end of it all, it would be something.

Head lamps swept through the gum trees. He dropped the butt on the floor and put his heel on it.

"She's here!"

The car skidded off the gravel, gained traction on the hoop of hardtop and stopped with its motor racing. He could see Gunilla's scarf as she leaned across and opened the doors of the car. She cut the head lamps leaving no more than amber disks shining and beeped the horn. Two long, one short. His heart reached out to her. Scared as she must be, she was making all the right moves. Kosky came close, his voice a hoarse whisper.

"Remember. They're out there watching. We're carrying a man who is sick. Make it look good and we're free."

He unlocked the front door, stepped back behind it as it opened. Darkness met darkness. The only sound coming from outside was that of the motor running. They grabbed Szily's body between them so that his right arm was laced over Hamilton's shoulders. Kosky was on the left, the fingers of his gun hand deep in the Baron's hair, pulling the dead man's head up and holding it in a semblance of life. They walked their burden forward, its feet scuffing over the ground in a travesty of voluntary movement.

Gunilla had brought the car as close as she could to the house, no more than twenty feet away. Hamilton kept his eyes on the shadows beyond, his skin crawling with expectancy. Surely they *had* to detect the deception. Any moment now and the game would be called. They went down the steps, the giant stone bears shielding them on both sides. But there was no attempt to stop them; no move from whoever was out there watching. They placed Szily's body carefully on the back seat. The Brazilian climbed in beside him and wiped the dead man's face with a handkerchief. The box of jade was on the seat between them. Hamilton reached over and switched on the head lamps. Light flooded through the gum trees. Gunilla just sat there staring up into the mirror. Her hands started to shake on the steering wheel.

"*Um Gottes Willen!*" she said in a shocked whisper.

Hamilton wrenched the mirror round, "Move it! Turn left when you get to the road."

The car jerked forward, scattering stones as the wheels dug into the graveled driveway. Gunilla barely slowed at the lodge and gunned through the gates.

"Easy!" he warned as she swung into the turn. He put his hand on her knee and gripped it hard. "Don't panic! Nobody touched him. It was heart failure."

She shook her head, peering through the windshield, her face drained of color. Hamilton turned. The road behind was clear. Szily's body had collapsed on the floor behind the driver's seat. The Brazilian glanced up from the open box in his lap. The jade seemed to fascinate him. Hamilton's hope was instinctive. The odds were still long against them making it to safety but they shortened with every yard covered.

"We'll have to get to a phone and warn Kohn."

Kosky closed the box without answering. Hamilton swung back to the girl.

"Where's your passport?"

She shook her head, "It's in the house but I don't care anymore."

She took the bend too sharply, plowing into the soft shoulder. He grabbed the padded dash, hanging on as she wrestled the car back on course.

"For crissakes!" he yelled.

She eased her foot on the gas pedal. "They can do what they like to me. I don't care anymore about anything."

She was crying now. The movement of his hand was instinctive. She drew away as far as she could.

"Don't touch me!" she warned sharply.

He turned around again, enlisting Kosky's help. "We've got to get to Kohn with the jade, don't you see it? He can prove that the Spreewald Collection is really his. That way we've got a chance."

The track where he'd left the motorbike was no more than half a mile away. The road behind was still empty, there was no sign of pursuit.

Kosky's small black eyes bored into his. Hamilton spoke with new enthusiasm.

"Listen, we've got to get to Kohn with the jade! I have a motorcycle stashed away. It'll carry the three of us to a cab then we make it to Kohn separately."

Kosky nodded. "Where is this motorcycle?"

"Coming up now!" He swung left toward Gunilla, pointing through the windshield to show her the turnoff.

The head lamps cut a swath of light in which the trees

flicked by. He winced as the end of Kosky's gun dug into the back of his neck. Suddenly he understood. Kosky was no one's man but his own. The pressure increased.

"Make a left and follow the wall," he said drearily.

He shut his eyes as the car rocked over the rough ground. They said the moment of truth came to everyone, but surely not like this. This bastard was going to murder them both in cold blood and there wasn't a thing he could do about it. Small animals disturbed by the car ran in the crevices of the wall. Dust rose and the clump of gorse grew nearer and nearer. Maybe the bike had been found. Everything else he had planned had gone sour.

"Hold it here," he said. Gunilla trod on the brakes. He nodded across at the yellow bushes by the wall. "In there."

"Switch off," said Kosky. There was no doubt that the gun menaced Gunilla as well as Hamilton. There was a kind of finality in everything that Kosky said. He made each order sound as if it would be the last. Kosky lowered the window and stared into the trees on his right.

The motor clattered on for a while then stopped. Gunilla was rocking from side to side, her face hidden in her hands. An old sad song played in Hamilton's mind but he still smiled. Habit was strong. He smiled without even knowing it.

"He's not going to put a hand on you," he said.

She looked up at him, wet-eyed. "It isn't your fault. It's nobody's fault but mine."

He didn't believe it but he was nonetheless grateful. "Nothing's going to happen," he said with false assurance.

"Take care!" Her voice was almost out of control.

"Out!" ordered Kosky.

He stepped over the dead man's body and marched Hamilton to the clump of gorse. The bike was still lying there, the cap and coveralls stuffed under the saddle. Hamilton lifted the machine and held it upright, bracing himself as Kosky lifted the gun.

"Start it!" the Brazilian ordered.

Hamilton kicked down hard. The stutter of the motor echoed through the trees.

"That's enough!" Kosky stepped nearer, peering down at the map that Hamilton had taped to the gas tank. He ripped it off and unfolded it. As he did so, Hamilton turned his head imperceptibly. It was impossible to see beyond the head lamps but he remembered that the car doors were open.

"Run!" he shouted, blocking Kosky's way with the motorbike. The next scene seemed to play in slow motion. The Brazilian floated away from the light in a crouch. Gunilla was off and running and almost into the trees. Kosky took aim, his left hand gripping his right wrist. The gun spat twice in rapid succession. The whine of the ricocheting shells followed the flat reports. Kosky trotted along the edge of the track, shading his eyes and searching the trees where Gunilla had disappeared. He stood stock-still, his head cocked, listening, but the woods were completely silent again. He came back into the light, bringing the acrid stink of the explosion with him.

Hamilton braced himself for what was coming. He'd watched it a thousand times on the screen, the red goo spreading on the chest of the two-dimensional heroes. Only this one was for real. Kosky's rubber soles had made crow's-foot tracks in the soft white dirt. Smoke curled from the slots in the silencer.

Kosky looked at Hamilton, the box of jade hugged under his left arm. Incredibly, he was still chewing.

"Whore's bastard!" he said and spat at the ground.

Hamilton lifted his head. It was weird the way everything seemed to be typecast, even down to the dialogue.

"Do what you have to do!"

Black snake eyes considered him from a dead white face. "What are you, a hero?" sneered Kosky. He jerked the gun back at the car. "Let the air out of the tires, all of it."

He stayed close, menacing Hamilton till the Ford settled down on the rims of its wheels. He leaned into the car, cut the lights and looked back once more at the woods.

"You're a fool," he said.

A nightjar shrieked discordantly. "She's out there somewhere," said Hamilton. "She's watching every move you make. You won't get away with it."

Kosky's arm streaked, grabbing the walkie-talkie with a force that broke the strap. He smashed it against the wall and threw what was left into the bushes. He marched Hamilton back to the bike, holding him there at point-blank range as he climbed into the coveralls. He pulled the cap low on his forehead. He spoke as if he drew on some evil force that could be directed at will and would prevail.

"Make for the Salazar Bridge and you better pray that we cross it. Because if we don't, my friend, you're dead!"

The words ballooned in Hamilton's mind. He realized that Kosky still needed him. *The Brazilian didn't know how to ride the machine!* It was as simple as that. Hamilton threw a leg over the saddle and kicked down on the starter. Kosky arranged himself on the pillion seat behind, the box of jade digging into Hamilton's shoulder blades. The gun was out of sight between their bodies. He operated the clutch with his toe and let the bike roll forward, avoiding the cart tracks. Kosky's touch on the trigger was light enough as it was. There'd still be traffic on the roads but all people would see would be a couple of men heading home. He forked right into the trees and gunned the small bike up the slope.

VIII

Machado put down the house phone. Years of command had instilled in him the certainty that his orders would be obeyed without question. But he had had to first threaten and finally plead to stop the groom from leading a frontal attack on the house. Now the entrance gates were open and Szily's men had been dispersed. The light in the Baron's bedroom had been extinguished, leaving the big house in absolute darkness. Szily was lucky to have had a heart attack. Braver men had learned the hard way with Kosky. Machado belched. His stomach was sour from the food he had eaten and the wine had parched his mouth. He emptied half a bottle of mineral water at a draft, considering the snub-nosed pistol on the bedside table. Only once had he killed a man and the memory still troubled him. He slipped the weapon in his pocket and dialed the veterinarian's number on the outside line. Cabral must have been standing close to the receiver. Machado gave his news grimly.

"They've got him, Luis."

Cabral's voice was aghast. "But how?"

"Does it matter how?" said Machado. "They've got him, that's all. He had some kind of a heart attack. They're demanding free passage for their car and no police intervention and they're taking him with them as hostage."

"Caramba!" The line sang in the ensuing silence. "So what now?"

"I've agreed to their terms. It's either that or they kill him. When they leave here I shall follow. It's all I can . . . wait a minute, I can hear the car coming now!"

Head lamps pierced the trees outside. He left the phone off the hook and ran to the window. The car made a U-turn and stopped. The driver dimmed the head lamps, leaving no more than a glow that faintly lit the front of the house. Machado opened the window and peered out. The two men emerged from beneath the porch supporting Szily between them. The Baron's head was high but he moved like a drunk, having to be lifted bodily into the back of the car. The head lamps were switched on to maximum and Machado saw the girl at the wheel. The car shot forward, spattering gravel as it hit the driveway. He watched it through the trees till the taillights disappeared. He picked up the phone again.

"They've taken the road to Cascais. Call headquarters

and have a block put on all frontier posts. And I want Kohn picked up, do you hear?"

"*Si,* Senhor!" He heard Cabral relay the instructions. The radio cars were in direct touch with Communications.

Machado cut in again. "And send one of your cars for a doctor. I don't care if they have to pull him out of his bed. Then follow me on the Cascais road. I'm leaving now."

He wrenched the door open and ran through the darkness. The only sound in the stableyard was the howling of the dogs and the stamping of the horses. He backed out the Renault, buckling a fender against a wall in his haste. He skidded into the loose gravel, scorched down to the gates and onto the road. It was fifteen kilometers to the first turnoff. Kosky's car couldn't be more than half that distance in front. Machado put his foot down hard on the gas pedal. Cabral wouldn't be far behind. The radio cars were geared for high speeds. He braked suddenly as a figure loomed in the headlights. The Renault slammed into the shoulder, shuddered and then regained traction. Gunilla Mayenfels was standing full in the path of the oncoming car, her arms in the air, her mouth open in an unheard scream. He rammed on the emergency brake, locking the wheels and bringing the car to a belated standstill. The girl's blazer was torn, her bell-bottomed trousers covered with pieces of bracken. Machado pulled the snub-nosed pistol from his pocket and threw the door open.

"Policia!"

She stumbled toward him and leaned against the door,

fighting for breath. He forced her chin up roughly. Her tear-streaked face was puffed, the backs of her hands scratched and bloodied.

"Where's Szily?" he demanded. "Where are the others?"

She looked at him blankly as if the questions were superfluous. "Szily is dead."

"You're lying," he said, grabbing her by the shoulders.

She shook her head helplessly. "He was dead when they brought him out of the house." She started to laugh, caught by hysteria, quietly at first and then louder.

He slapped her face once, a hard stinging slap that shocked her back to reality.

He pointed at the seat beside him. "Get in."

She did as he said, sitting with her knees together, her hands folded in her lap like a small girl who has been chastised.

"The truth," he said firmly. "I want the truth and quickly."

He heard her out with growing distaste. He'd been bluffed like some fresh-faced recruit from the country. The sound of a car coming up fast behind echoed along the road. Head lamps illuminated the forest. The radio car slammed broadside-on to a stop. Cabral pounded over behind his shadow, his good hand holding his gun at the ready. He looked from the girl to Machado, his long narrow face questioning. Machado's voice was tight.

"I'm sick of Kosky, Luis. Szily was already dead when they carried him out of the house. His body is in the car. There's a track up the road where the boundary wall curves."

Cabral's jaw muscles tightened. "And the others?"

"On a motorcycle heading for the Salazar Bridge. The girl heard Kosky talking. She was hiding. He was going to kill her but she ran."

Cabral spread his legs, glancing in curiously at Gunilla. She met his look calmly, her mouth and eyes now controlled. She started to clean her face.

"The doctor's on his way," said Cabral. "He should be here in five or six minutes."

The driver of the radio car had moved the vehicle to the side of the road. Machado drew in his gut and eased himself from behind the wheel.

"I'm taking your car; it's faster. I want you to stay here till the doctor comes." He pointed at the phone under the dash. "Call me as soon as he's seen Szily."

Cabral's expression was doubtful. "With respect, Senhor Cabo . . . "

Machado brushed past. "Respect, your aunt's ass. Get those men out of that car!"

The girl came running after him, grabbing his arm and bringing him to a standstill.

"Take me with you! Please, I have to come!"

He tried to shake her off but she clung tight, resisting his effort. Cabral caught her from behind and lifted her. He cursed as she kicked, connecting with his shin.

"Put her down," ordered Machado.

"Please!" she said again, her hand on Machado's sleeve again. "Don't you see that I *have* to come?"

He probed deep into her face. "This man is your lover?"

She looked from one man to the other, meeting Cabral's ironical smile with head erect.

"No, but he saved my life."

Machado nodded. "Get in the car."

Cabral walked away, his back stiff with disapproval. He barked an order and four men piled out of the police vehicle, standing in silence as Machado pushed the girl in the back. He took the wheel and picked up the radiophone. A staccato voice answered. Machado identified himself.

"Red Flash! Alert the guard post at the south end of the Salazar Bridge. Two men riding tandem on a motorcycle. Detain and hold. Dangerous. Over and out."

Cabral leaned his head through the open window, his voice for Machado alone.

"You're stubborn and given to lapses of judgment but you are not expendable. Kosky is. Remember that and take no chances."

Machado started the motor. "And you remember this, put a guard on the museum, it's national property!" He floored the gas pedal and the souped-up car shot forward, head lamps reaching out into the darkness. Trees and walls flashed by and then there was open space. He kept the car in the center of the road, his hand near the switch that controlled the police siren. The escape route that Kosky had chosen offered a chance to reach the bridge before he did. Machado forked left at the crossroads. The car barreled through sleeping villages, past the stark outline of the tobacco factory and into the hills behind Estoril. A few more minutes and they'd be on the autostrada. He looked up into the driving mirror. The girl was leaning forward, her hands on the back of his seat, steadying herself as the car swayed on the bends. He could no longer tell with people of her age, still less with foreigners, but she seemed to be unabashed, without shame. He spoke on impulse, the words blunt.

"How could you rob a man who befriended you?"

She took her hands away as if they had been scalded. "If the man was Szily, easily. Or perhaps you don't know, Inspector?"

"Know what?" he said. The road ahead unwound like a tube of black toothpaste.

"That he betrayed my father."

The hates and loves of children were centered on their parents for so long in their lives. It was better perhaps to have no child than to see it end like this. The rule of silence no longer seemed to apply and he broke it deliberately.

"All I know about your father is that he died on the night of May seven, nineteen forty-five."

It was a brutal speech and he regretted it as soon as he had spoken. The high-pitched whine of the motor increased as the car made the long ascent through the black umbrella pines. The lights of Lisbon showed clear in the distance. It was some time before she answered. Her voice was quiet and resigned.

"Of course. I always guessed, I suppose, secretly. But at least he died honorably."

Machado belched. The dumplings he had eaten were still sitting heavily on his stomach.

"What's that supposed to mean?"

She leaned forward again, her breath on the back of his neck. "The Spreewald Collection. You must know about it. You know everything else. Szily had it. That's what they took tonight."

A car flicked by. There was no sign of the men he was hunting. Memory assembled the pieces in place and the old files he had read took on new meaning. He'd been used, hoodwinked, right from the start. By the Inspector of Cause, the Minister, everyone—including Szily himself with the nonsense about his paintings.

"And this Jew from London?"

"The jade was his father's. The Nazis stole it. All Hamilton was doing was getting it back for him. Kosky betrayed them both. Those things are evil. Everyone who touches them suffers in some way."

He heard but his mind was busy in other directions. This girl was the only one who had spoken the truth. The circumstances put it beyond doubt. The key was the jade. Governments would argue about its ownership. The Germans would certainly be involved and the British would probably add weight to Kohn's claim. If the case ever came to court, skilled advocates would twist the law, arguing the absurdity of stealing one's own property which was what Kohn appeared to be doing. And, by extension, Hamilton as his agent. After thirty years of it, Machado knew the rules of the game well enough. Ministers had no stomach for international argument. Doors would close mysteriously in his face. The Inspectors of Cause would make their bland denials of responsibility. He'd be left on his own to explain, his hands tied behind his back and a clamp on his tongue. But none of it mattered as long as Kosky didn't escape.

The girl's fingers touched his shoulder. "*Please,* Inspector! He's not a bad man."

He took his eyes off the road long enough to see her face in the mirror. A man could father a girl like this, surround her with love and understanding only to see her destroy her life.

"He's a convicted thief," he said pointedly.

Her fingers moved along his shoulder. "Help him. I don't care what you do to me but help him."

The Salazar Bridge was a string of lights in the darkness over the river. Machado was not impressed with its technical magic. His belief was in the land and the people who worked it, the women who saved bread and washed their clothes in streams, the goatherds on the mountains, the young who kept the old ways. These people were Portugal. They knew it instinctively with no dreams of grandeur, content with their own horizons.

He held the wheel one-handed, slowed and used the radiophone. Communications linked his call with headquarters of the Guarda Nacional. The news was negative. Twenty men had been posted at the south exit from the bridge but no motorcycle had passed within the last thirty-five minutes. He hung up and asked to be connected with Cabral's radio car. It was seven kilometers behind and coming up fast. He finished the call and spoke over his shoulder.

"One worry less for you. Your friend is no murderer. Szily died from a massive coronary. The doctor says death would have been instantaneous."

She half-whispered something that he neither heard nor cared about. His interest was in Kosky, not the Canadian.

But if a lamb lay down with a wolf it was just too bad. At the end of the last long slope the autostrada merged with a network of avenues spiraling into the city. Off to the left the aqueduct soared, gray-pink in the glow from the street lamps. The signs followed one another rapidly. *Praça d'Espanha. Ponte Salazar.* He swung right, looking for a place to put the car out of sight. The bridge was half a kilometer distant. Whatever traffic used it was bound to come this way. He pulled off the road, the radio car jolting across rubble into the shadows of a half-finished building. The ground was littered with plumbing fixtures and sacks of cement. He cut his head lamps, stopped and used the radiophone again, giving headquarters his exact location.

"Put your window down," he said to Gunilla. He wanted to hear every sound.

She used both hands to do it, frowning with concentration. Her clothes had been brushed clean and her scarf retied. A plane droned overhead, on its way to Portela, wing lights flashing. The approach to the bridge was illiminated by powerful arc lamps. Substance and shadow were as sharply defined as the perimeter of a concentration camp. A truck piled with oranges lumbered toward the city, the smell of the fruit sweetening the air. Gunilla watched it disappear.

"I'm not afraid of you," she said suddenly in a low voice.

He turned his head. The statement gave him a perverse sort of pleasure. "What *are* you afraid of?"

Her mouth and eyes were nervous. "Do you believe in prayer, Inspector?"

"Prayer?" he repeated.

She nodded quickly. "People talk to God and believe that He listens."

He stared out across the river at the enormous concrete Christ. The price of its vulgarity would have endowed a small hospital.

"I think I am out of practice," he said. "Why?"

Her chin came up. "Because I'm praying for Hamilton's life. *That's* what I'm afraid for."

Machado shifted the cheroot, cocking his head so that his ears were attuned to the night. A cat screamed high in the rocks behind. A tug hooted somewhere out in the estuary. Gradually he detected a sharper note against the dull grumble of the city. He wiped his forehead surreptitiously. Gunilla was sitting up straight, her eyes fixed on the underpass.

"Down!" Machado said suddenly.

She went down quickly, crouching behind the seat. He pulled the snub-nosed revolver from his jacket pocket and put it on the seat beside him. Cabral leaned from the window of the other car, holding up his thumb. Machado nodded.

The noise was louder now, like calico squares being ripped apart at high speed. Seconds later, the motorcycle chugged into the glare of the overhead lamps and passed in front of the building site. The Canadian was sitting up stiffly and, clinging to him, Kosky in cap and coveralls. They were near enough for Machado to interpret the awkwardness of their positions. Kosky had a gun pointing at Hamilton's back. The motorcycle clattered onto the metal runway. Machado turned the ignition key. The two cars lurched out of the shadows in pursuit, one on each side of the bridge. They traveled slowly, keeping their distance behind the bike, their headlights on maximum. The cortege was halfway over the bridge when gray-clad figures swarmed out of the tollbooths at the far end. Kosky saw them and raised himself, one hand on Hamilton's shoulder. His other hand held a gun. Machado spoke into the built-in bullhorn.

"Both of you stop with your hands in the air!"

Kosky swung around and took deliberate aim. A shell sang through the steel girders. The two cars kept going inexorably. Hamilton wrenched the handlebars and the motorbike swerved violently. It mounted the center strip and buckled, spilling both men in a flurry of arms and legs. Kosky was first up, leaving the Canadian crawling on hands and knees. The bike was rotating like a dying wasp, drive-wheel spinning. Kosky backed off from the glare of the advancing headlights, looking from the cars to the uniformed police pounding along the bridge toward him. He fired again, shattering the windshield of Cabral's car. Another shot plowed through the bodywork.

Cabral poked the snout of his submachine gun through the broken windshield.

"No!" yelled Machado. He wanted this man alive. He burst the door open as Kosky started to climb up the girders. Hamilton's leap missed the Brazilian's foot by inches. Kosky hauled himself up and stood on top of the parapet, hugging a box against his chest. He faced the river like a parachutist about to make a free fall and then plunged forward, describing a lazy somersault. By the time Machado reached the spot, there was nothing to see in the deep swift water, seventy meters below. He pulled his head back sharply, massaging his teeth with his tongue. There were seven recorded suicides from the bridge. All had their necks broken. Kosky's body would wash up somewhere along the sandy wastes of Caparica, face, hands and genitals eaten by crabs. He shook his head, glancing down at the river. Strange how a personal defeat became a public victory. The world had been rid of a savage and dangerous animal. Another closed file would be added to the pile in the storeroom under the eaves at headquarters.

Hamilton was standing by the fallen motorcycle, his hands in the air. Machado pushed him over to the car, spread his legs and went through his pockets. He threw the contents on the front seat of the car and beckoned to a plainclothesman. The cop sat in the back, separating Hamilton from the girl. Machado walked over to Cabral and the two men moved away. Cabral had already dismissed the uniformed men, who were heading back toward the exit.

Machado spat the dead cheroot from his mouth, looking out at the river.

"Any casualties?"

Cabral's eyes quizzed him. "A few cuts. Nothing serious. We lost the bastard. I'm sorry."

Machado didn't want to talk about it. "What happened with Kohn?"

"They're holding him at headquarters."

Machado glanced across at the spot where Kosky had fallen. Someone was chalking the girder and the ground in front.

"I want you to do something for me, Luis."

Cabral's thin face was alert and understanding. "Whatever you wish, old friend, you know that."

"Yes, I know it," Machado agreed. Flashbulbs popped. One of Cabral's men was taking photographs of the bridge and the motorcycle. Machado loosened his tie and looked up. Cabral topped him by five inches.

"I want you to get rid of all this shit and go home to bed."

Cabral's shoulder rose. "Just like that? There are still bars that are open, remember. Drink a coffee with me and talk."

"There's nothing to talk about." Machado yawned and rubbed his knuckles through the thatch of gray hair. "It's gone three. You can leave me your driver."

Cabral beckoned the man over. Machado sat next to him, Hamilton's belongings in his lap. Cabral saluted.

"Goodnight, Senhor Cabo!"

Machado lifted a hand as the car went into a U-turn. Cabral would accept his decisions whatever they were. The unused revolver sagged in Machado's pocket. At the back of his mind he still felt cheated. Kosky's end had been in a sense an escape. Only a few shards of glass and some chalkmarks on the girders remained as evidence. Machado picked the envelope from the pile on his knee. Inside were two carbon copies of a typewritten statement, one in Portuguese, the other in German. Both had been initialed in the appropriate places.

I, Freiherr Dieter von Szily, acknowledge the receipt of five jeweled jade figures known as THE SPREEWALD COLLECTION, undertaking to hold and preserve the said SPREEWALD COLLECTION in my charge until such time as its return is requested by an accredited official of the German government.

Signed at Penha Longa, May 7, 1945

D. V. S.

He stuffed the sheets of paper back in the envelope. The original must have been burned with Gunilla's father. He turned toward her, holding the envelope between his thumb and forefinger.

"Perhaps God does listen."

She took the envelope. Her eyes hurried over the typed sentences then she looked past the plainsclothesman at Hamilton. Machado sighed. He was fifty-four years old, bucktoothed and probably about to make a fool of himself.

False dawn was breaking. The city was in illumination from the sky as well as the street lamps. A new day had already started along the waterfront. Fishing boats were nosing their way through the rusted freighters. Crane booms swung in the fierce white glare of overhead lights. Bare-footed men with baskets on their heads trotted across streetcar tracks. Cats prowled among the garbage cans. Hamilton groped for a cigarette but the inspector had taken them with the rest of his belongings. He winced, feeling the pain in his side where the bike had fallen on top of him. He had a sense of having done all this before, disastrously. From jail to jail in two different countries within the space of three days. It was probably some sort of record.

Gunilla hadn't looked at him since she'd read the contents of the envelope he had found. The plainclothesman sitting between them had the sort of face that discouraged conversation. They sat in a silence broken only by the whine of the tires on the cobblestones. He still had no more than a basic understanding of what was happening but one thing was sure and certain. He was in deep trouble. More than that, he had a shrewd idea that a request to see a lawyer or the consul would never get off the ground. Here they played by different rules.

The police car climbed a steep hill and turned right, stopping outside a large dark building. A few lighted windows dotted the gloomy façade. A couple of uniformed men armed with machine guns guarded the entrance. Machado said something in Portuguese and the cop touched Hamilton's knee. He pulled himself together. A cell here would be much like a cell anywhere else. He followed Machado into a lofty hall, its peeling plaster lit by naked bulbs. Gunilla was close behind with the plainclothesman. They were halfway across the hall when Hamilton saw Kohn, sitting handcuffed on a bench, staring at the ground. Another plainclothesman watched him from the wall. They joined the group from the car, Kohn dragging his feet as if his legs already carried a ball and chain. The clock on the wall showed twenty minutes of four.

Machado led them in Indian file along a succession of whitewashed corridors, past vague recesses smelling of carbolic acid, and took a stone flight of stairs. He signaled for Kohn's handcuffs to be removed. Their escorts ranged themselves along the wall. Machado opened a door. Gunilla, Kohn and Hamilton sat down on a sofa in the office. Her hand crept into his and he was glad of it. He'd seen two men die within hours and the future echoed with the clank of keys and the slamming of cell doors.

Machado took the chair behind the desk and switched on a goosenecked lamp. It lit the top half of his body, catching the toothy gleam and chestnut eyes as he arranged Hamilton's belongings in two piles. Money, tickets and passport went in the center of the blotter, the burglar tools, walkie-talkie and hotel key to one side. He rolled his eyes along the sofa and tapped himself on the chest.

"Inspector Machado."

Hamilton smiled weakly. *"Me injun, you white man. You no go Guadeloupe!"*

Gunilla's fingers tightened on his hand as Machado's expression changed. The Inspector fired his words like an angry chipmunk. Gunilla interpreted. "He says that you lack respect!"

Hamilton shook his head painfully. "A man thinks of something funny, he smiles. I meant no offense." He stared at the wall pointedly.

Machado continued, addressing his words to Kohn. Gunilla said, "They're going to take you to the airport and put you on the first plane for London."

Hamilton raised his head again. Kohn cleared his throat but no words came. He had aged in the last few hours. He was nothing more than an old fat man in rumpled clothes. His voice rasped desperately.

"The Spreewald Collection. Ask what happens now. I have the right to know."

Orange streaked the sky beyond the painted windows. Machado doodled with an old-fashioned fountain pen as

Gunilla put the question. He answered courteously but firmly. Gunilla turned to Kohn.

"He says he never heard of the Spreewald Collection."

Hamilton cut Kohn's protest short. "It's at the bottom of the river with Kosky. For crissakes, don't you see what he's doing? He's giving you an out. Take it!"

Machado called. One of the plainclothesmen outside poked his head around the door and beckoned. Kohn heaved himself up ponderously. He looked down, touching Gunilla's cheek with his fingertips.

"I'm sorry," he said. The apology was for them both.

"That's life," said Hamilton. "About the money. I guess I never really earned it."

Kohn turned from the doorway, hands lifting expressively as he looked at Gunilla, then the door closed behind him.

Machado yawned, retracting his lips over his prominent teeth. He pushed the passport, tickets and money across the desk in Hamilton's direction.

"Pick them up," whispered Gunilla.

He did so as in a dream. Machado yawned again and glanced at his watch. His voice was pitched too low to be heard outside the room. Gunilla's grip tightened again on Hamilton's fingers. She spoke, with her eyes on Machado's face.

"He's letting you go. You'll be kept downstairs in the cells till the train leaves for Paris."

It was a good sixty seconds before the words made sense. "What will they do to you?"

She shrugged, her eyes smudged with fatigue but her

smile ready. "Nothing. I think he must have read Shakespeare. 'A plague on both your houses.' "

A plainclothesman peered around the door and they both stood. "Goodbye," Hamilton said. "It's been a good one."

She felt in her purse and produced an envelope. For a moment he thought it was the one he had taken from the safe. But it was bigger and fatter. He lifted the flap.

"It's the rest of the money," she said. "Kohn wanted it that way." She pushed the envelope inside his coat.

Machado was doodling again on the blotter, his head bent. "Thanks," said Hamilton.

Her mouth was uncertain. "Isn't it ever going to stop for you? Are you always going to be running?"

He lifted a shoulder and glanced down at her. "I guess. Unless I remember how to walk."

She reached up, took his face between her hands and kissed him full on the mouth.

"Don't forget me, Scott."

Hamilton looked away to the man at the desk. Machado's head was up, his expression unreadable.

"I won't forget you," Hamilton promised.

The noise of his feet on the stone stairs followed him along the empty corridor.